THE PRINCIPAL

JOSEPH SCHUMACHER

1.

"Perfection exists. It is not some abstract concept that great people spend their entire lives trying to reach but never actually attaining. That is a lie perpetuated by the weak-willed and cowardly in order to make failure acceptable. Not only can you make your school perfect, but you can maintain this state of perfection indefinitely. You can literally make your school into a heaven. In <u>The Principal's Guide to Success</u> I will show you how."

My name is Principal Kent. I am the Principal. It's early on Monday and school just started. I'm making my rounds around the school, greeting students and faculty, popping into classrooms and seeing how everyone is doing. A school is like one enormous, endlessly elaborate machine, and part of my job as Principal is to grease and clean every cog and belt to make sure it runs as smoothly as possible.   I step into the first classroom, Douglas Holt's first period Biology class. Holt's a good man. He's forty-five and not married but that doesn't interfere with his teaching as far as I can tell. I have the code for his voicemail so I know he doesn't have much luck with women because they leave a lot of angry messages on his school phone. I know a lot about Holt because I know a lot about every teacher in this school. I know what bar he frequents. I know he's one of the few people that still rents his pornography from a video store.

I say hello to the students. Since they are a fresh and well-cultivated group of freshman almost all of them answer me back. Only Mike Black and Olivia Taylor stay silent. I make a mental note to keep a closer eye on those two; they could be harboring subversive thoughts. It's important to stop these thoughts before they become behaviors. As a Principal a wide variety of correctional tools are at my disposal, but I hope I won't need to use them. They should both go to the rally tomorrow for the football game against Lincoln High. Nothing removes subversive thoughts like an injection of pure school spirit. It makes a person better when they take pride in belonging to something larger than themselves.

There's a midterm today and the class quiets down as the tests are passed out. In my opinion, there's nothing more peaceful, gratifying and beautiful than the moment of silence before a test. The students are no longer nervous about it now that it's sitting in front of them. All their energy is set in anticipation of the task ahead. Every student made equal, focusing on the same papers, thinking the same thoughts. For an instant thirty young minds are made into a single silent entity. If I could prolong the moment forever I would.

Next, I walk down the hallway and up the stairs to Classroom 203, Peter Volker's metalshop class. I find that vocational classes are a necessity. Not everyone is able to memorize biological facts or grasp abstract concepts. Some students are just better with their hands than their higher reasoning skills. What's important is that these students still find something to focus on, to put effort into. Who knows, they'll probably be making more money sooner than most of the students in this school, and they won't have any student loans to pay off.

Pete's a good teacher. He looks mean enough and has enough missing fingers to keep students in line through sheer presence. Maybe he doesn't pay close enough attention to the students, but as long as he continues to maintain discipline I don't mind. Whether it's fear or respect, all that matters is that he can control the masses. Currently Ray's reading a copy of Soldier of Fortune magazine and occasionally grunting at students to quiet down.

I scan the room full of drill presses, circular saws, and grinding wheels. Most students are actively engaged in the metalworking process. I wave to Stan Birch, a sophomore and starting tackle for the football team. He's got his arm around Michelle Fowler, and I can tell that they've had intercourse. I make a mental note to add them to the network in my office. I need to watch those two closely to make sure their relationship is solid, I don't need my starting tackle struggling with relationship troubles when he should be focused on winning the game. Beating Lincoln High is all that matters.

A boy in the back corner next to the grinder catches my eye. Sparks cascade off the small piece of metal he has in his hands. Daniel Slater, junior. Shy around girls but loaded with testosterone, he's someone I like to make sure is directing his hormone-fueled energy in a positive way. Good kid, creative, but prone to verbal altercations. I step behind him.

"Hi Daniel."

He jumps, and turns around. He tries too late to hide the object he's fabricating. "What's that, Daniel?"

Daniel sighs, resigned to his fate. "A throwing star."

"Yes, a shuriken. Hand it over, please." It's a polished square of metal with four sharp-edged, pointed triangles extending from each corner. It's actually very well crafted and extremely keen.

"Now Daniel, you remember the school's policy when it comes to weapons."

"But I spent a week making that! I want to see if it works at least!"

"Well... I do have to confiscate this."

Daniel's face falls.

"Okay. We'll give it one test run," I say. I can tell by Daniel's reaction that I have one more loyal fan. Loyalty is important in a school like this. Positive public opinion is another kind of grease I use to keep my school operating smoothly under my control.

I pick up a thick board of plywood and stand it against the door. Some students are watching me now. Better make this quick.

"Pete, I'm going to, uh, demonstrate some applied functions of metal fabrication."

He grunts and doesn't look up from his magazine.

I wind back and throw the star at the board from across the room. It spins into a blur, cutting through the air with a hiss. Thwack! It hits the plywood, continues through and embeds itself halfway into the door.

4

"Sick!" shouts Daniel.

"No more making lethal weapons please," I say, and place the shuriken in my pocket.

As I make my way from Mr. Volker's class to my office I run into my Vice Principal, Chris Hasty. Chris is a very good VP to have. Promoting him from substitute teacher to administration in just four years has instilled in him a sense of duty and obligation that I have come to depend on. I could sense his extreme intellect from day one by the way he micromanaged the very first class he taught. Now, with Chris keeping busy running the more technical aspects of administrative duties, I can focus on what I feel to be most important: how the lives of my students are shaped, hour by hour, period by period.

"Mr. Kent-"

"Adam, please."

"Yes, Adam, sorry. I'd like to go over the details of our budget revisions, and also the private donations we've received for the month, including those anonymous ones." I mentally gloss over all of this. But then, Chris says: "And the security camera man is here."

I don't tell anyone this, but I donate nearly my entire salary each month to the school in the form of anonymous donations. It makes the budget easier to handle on an accounting level, and since I have strict control over how the budget is allocated it ultimately goes to improving the school. Specifically, I've been setting aside a portion of funding off the books for years to purchase a top-of-the-line security system. I've had to reduce my spending in aspects of my life outside the school, but it's worth every penny. The more closely I can monitor my students, the more closely I can oversee their movements and behaviors and become a larger positive force in their lives. Not only that, but my eyes will be able to see the entire hallway system and outside grounds at once and strike quickly and accurately at any subversive anti-establishment activities. I've looked forward to this day for a long time.

"Put a copy of the budget on my desk, Chris."

"I did sir, last week."

"Well, right now I have a pretty full schedule, so how about you do what you have to do to the budget, and I'll approve it. Gotta go now, but I'll see you later." I quickly leave Chris before he can object, and I dance down the south hallway to the reception area.

Inside, vainly attempting to flirt with the office ladies, is a man dressed in jeans, a button up shirt, a white hat with "Vanguard Electronics" across the front and a clipboard in his hand.

I walk up to him and shake his other hand. "Hello. My name is Principal Kent. I am the Principal. You must be here to install the surveillance system."

"Yes sir. I'm Roger. I see you ordered the 'Big Brother' full service package. Personally, these are my favorite kind of system to install. Infra-red, high def, external hard drives for weeks of feed storage. Enclosed in tempered glass with a minute profile to protect the lens and reduce visibility. This is the good stuff."

"Good to hear. I'd like to give you a tour of the school, so I can show you where to put the cameras. Let's take a walk."

The first things you see when you walk through the front glass double doors at the entrance to the school is our mascot, an anthropomorphized Tasmanian Tiger, jaws stretched impossibly wide. In a glass case along the west wall are rows of trophies, in chronological order. I am proud of the fact that there are more trophies from my ten years as Principal than in the rest of the school's entire existence. It reminds me of the game against our hated rivals, Lincoln High, scheduled for tonight. Hand drawn posters adorn the east wall, announcing dances and club activities.

"Two here, wide angle, facing the entrance and down the hall," I say. Roger nods.

We amble down the main hall as students stream past on their way to fourth period. I high five Jacob Green, tight end on the football team. Every bit of positive reinforcement is important, especially on game day. Especially against Lincoln High, that team of thick-skulled mouth breathers.

I point out where I want cameras: inside the cafeteria, outside the band room, high on the ceiling in the gymnasium. One in each hallway junction. Outside the main building, a cluster in a fan pattern to view the entirety of the quad and courtyard. One at the pool and two trained on each parking lot. One in the library. I want cameras overlooking the basketball courts, the tennis courts, the baseball diamond, and the football field. I want cameras around the entire perimeter of the school. I have planned the placement of these cameras for years, utilizing each one to cover as much of the campus as possible. Already I can feel my line of sight expanding exponentially. I will be able to keep such a good eye on my students.

Finally, I finish my tour back where we started. "So, Roger, how long will this take?" I begin, when I see the Principal of Lincoln High, Linda Chu, stride through the doors. I'm not fond of the woman. In my opinion she sees teachers as efficient tools for developing human capital. I don't. Not as efficient, or as human capital. I fondle the shuriken in my pocket, tracing its edge with my finger.

"Hello Linda," I say warmly, firmly shaking her hand.

"Adam! Just stopping by before the big game tonight. I'm sure you've been playing up the whole 'rivalry' business. Me too. All in good fun, of course."

"Yes, fun." I don't tell her how I plan to work the student body into a frothing frenzy of school pride at the rally today. I want them to call for Lincoln High's blood. Nothing unites a group like a common enemy, and Lincoln High is definitely that. "Keeping your students in your seats?"

"Yes, as well as I can. I'm interested in how you're preparing for the standardized tests coming up. I'm sure you're aware state funding is tied to how well your students perform."

I could care less about how well my students fill in bubbles. What's the point of making sure my school ranks near the top in attendance statewide if they spend their days preparing for a test that has nothing to do with the unique community that I've spent so long fostering? Money? No, money is nowhere on my priority list.

My mouth forms a smile. "Oh, you know. A little of this, a little of that. I'm focusing on the shape of their circles, you know, making sure they're penciling consistently solid and inside the lines."

"I see. You know, it may not seem like it on the surface, but there's actually a lot of benefits to devoting time to making sure students meet the state requirements. Money, for one. And we are State schools, not private institutions. Your vision and the state's vision of the form your curriculum takes don't have to be in conflict. "

I clench my teeth. They're not the state's students. They're my students. I and I alone am responsible for their well being and educational experience. "Well, I appreciate your concern. However, I think your time would be better spent not worrying about how I run my school, but rather on making sure you play your hardest today. Make sure your team is hydrated and follows the rules of engagement."

Principal Chu laughs. "Same to you, Adam. I'm glad we're talking like this. I'd be happy to debate with you more the merits of focusing on human capital rather than-"

"Ah, I'd be glad to talk more with you but I'm afraid Roger and I-" I put my arm around the technician's shoulders, "have some pressing business. I'll see you at the game... friend."

We walk back to the reception area. Roger's clipboard is full of notes and diagrams. "It shouldn't take me and my team more than three days. Once I place the cameras, I need to connect them all to the same feed and start them recording. Do you have a monitor room picked out?"

As a matter of fact, I do. A former storage closet, across the hall from my office, next to the evidence room. I let Frank inside.

"Great! When I'm done this wall will be lined with video monitors, each with a rotating live feed of your cameras. With the hard drives, you have enough disk space to store a week's worth of recordings. You can rewind on any screen, at any time."

I shiver with pleasure. "Well, I'll leave you to it. If any students ask what you're doing, tell them you're putting in a new sprinkler system. I don't want them to know I'm watching, not at first."

It's now fifth period. I talk with sophomore Amy Portier as she passes by, making sure she's studying for her upcoming midterm and is practicing her flute for the wind ensemble's concert on Friday. I take a vested interest in every student's life. As long as they're in my school, they are under my protection and guidance. The good students are, anyway. The bad ones are closely watched, grouped together and separated from the larger, positively contributing student body to limit the psychic damage they can inflict.

I take this time to enter my evidence room. It's a spacious room with no windows and charcoal carpeting, filled wall to wall with shelves. The shelves are stocked with contraband I've confiscated from recidivist offenders who attempt to challenge my authority over their materials. The illicit fruits from eight years of confiscation fill every inch of shelving. Pornographic magazines. Spray paint. Obscene T-shirts. Sling shots. Airsoft guns. Butterfly knives. Fart machines and whoopee cushions. Prescription pills. Cigarettes. Beer. Vodka disguised in water bottles. Brass knuckles. Steel meat tenderizer knuckles. Baseball bats.

And now, a throwing star.

In the back corner rests a cork billboard studded with pink and blue pushpins connected with string. Each pin represents a male or female student, and they are connected by string to another student they've had intimate relations with. I hear enough gossip, scan enough confiscated notes, and read enough body language to have diagrammed a good portion of my school's sexual network.

Now there's nothing wrong with my students exploring their physical desires. However, I've found that the diagram is a very useful tool. Sometimes I need to figure out the motives behind a lunchtime fistfight, and the clues are usually in the blue and pink pins. Sometimes a cold starts going around the school and if I can tell who's kissing who I can quickly and effectively quarantine the infected. In the event of a more serious sickness my network will save lives. I add a pin for Stan Birch and connect it to Michelle's pin, which is already the nexus of several strings.

It's my job as Principal to protect the students, and I can best fulfill this duty by knowing the students better than they know themselves. The more I know and understand, the better a position I can act from. That's how I've maintained power and control in this school for so long, by gaining knowledge. And also giving preferred parking permits to the right people in order to gain their trust.

I take a moment to enjoy the silence and collect my thoughts, preparing for the upcoming rally only minutes away. I have so many things planned. A cheerleader performance, the band playing energetic musical numbers, a competitive balloon popping game between seniors and juniors. And all of it a call to arms against the Lincoln High oppressors. I need to make sure the students have a fun diversion from their normal school day, but also make it obvious to them that it is very, very important that we win this football game. I can't understate the paramount importance of the match. It's more than a game. It's a struggle for scholastic supremacy. I decide that a certain amount of slander against Lincoln High's students, faculty, and cafeteria food is required.

I leave the room, flushed with energy, and am about to march to the gymnasium ahead of the crowd when something lying on the ground catches my eye: folded paper with printed writing.

Litter of some kind? I have a personal vendetta against littering. The visual impact of a clean school on visitors and residents alike is important to me. But no matter how many times I tell these people that littering is the ultimate uncivilized act, even when the trash can is only ten feet away from them, it continues to happen. Even though I give my janitorial force high pay and Jewish holidays off, one or two pieces like this sneak through.

I pick it up and almost ball it up when large type catches my eye: **BAYVIEW HIGH SCHOOL GAZETTE**.

Below it, the headline reads "PRINCIPAL KENT WINS LOTTERY, BUYS SECURITY CAMERAS."

No byline with the author's name.

It's hard for my eyes to focus enough to read the rest of the article. Lies. Slander. Treason. The ultimate trespass, the ultimate obscene gesture against authority. The authors of this newsletter must be found. They must be made to answer for their crimes. Their distribution must be stopped.

My hands are trembling. I take a deep breath, then another. "First the rally," I whisper to myself. "The troops must be supported. Morale must be high. With that comes victory on the field over Lincoln High." The paper clenched tightly in my hand, I go to address the crowd.

The brass band plays the theme from Terminator, rotating their bodies back and forth in time with the music. The bleachers are filled with students talking, laughing, shoving each other and stomping their feet to the music. Danny Hock, dressed up in a plush representation of our mascot, does cartwheels and head spins. The security guards stand at the doorways, scanning the crowd with their arms crossed as is appropriate but also tapping their feet in time with the band.

I approach the podium, soaking in the energy and excitement. I raise my hands for silence. It takes a while, but eventually the students yield to my authority and silence falls over the gym. I still have that power, at least. I still receive the respect I demand.

"Students of Bayview High School," I begin. "Freshmen. Sophomores. Juniors. Seniors. I have tried to make this rally fun. We have excellent music. Friendly balloon popping competitions. Soon, the lovely Bayview High cheerleaders will perform an enticing dance for our enjoyment. But we mustn't let these festivities lull us into a false sense of security. It's all fun and games now, but in two hours it will be anything but. You see, there is one mistake today we cannot make. We cannot treat our match tonight as a game. A competition, yes. But this is not a game. This is a war. Tonight, we will take the field of battle, and we will leave victorious!

"I will not lie. Out enemy is devious. They will bend the rules until they break, using every underhanded trick at their disposal to see that we fail. They have no honor. Lincoln High players are less than dogs. I will not lie. Our enemy is fierce. Their athletic department has been pouring buckets of money into their team. They spend indiscriminately on equipment, trainers, illegal steroids and experimental medical procedures. Biological muscle enhancement. Leg lengthening. Adrenaline shots. They have been conditioned to hate us. Do not show them any love, because they will respond with none. Lincoln High players are beings of pure darkness.

"But do not lose heart. Tonight, we meet on the field as equals. They have the best team money can buy. But we have what money can't buy. Heart. Determination. Honor. Steve Ortiz's throwing arm. It's not the size of the dog in the fight, as you well know. It's the size of the fight in the dog. And our dog, the last Tasmanian Tiger in the wild, has bigger jaws than anyone else. Our team will not back down. We will not falter. And we will not fail.

"But the team needs our support. They need to know that every head and heart in the stadium is with them. United under a common cause, with a common soul. Nothing will divide us. We are legion, and at the same time, we are one.

"They need to see us support them. They need to see our shirts and sweaters emblazoned with the Bayview High Football logo, available for purchase in the student store. They need to see us waving Bayview High Football banners, foam fingers, and matching hats. I'd like to take this moment to thank our sponsors Korben Paint and Tile and Thompson Realty for their generous donations, and all the other businesses whose names appear on our scoreboard.

"Are we going to beat Lincoln High? I can't hear you! I said, are we going to murder Lincoln High? Are we going to litter the field with their bones? Are we going to kill their descendants and wipe their seed from the face of the earth? Will we win this war?

"Yes we will."

I pause, and let the wild cheering wash over my body. "Remember, this is not a game. Thank you. Now let's hear it for the Bayview High cheerleading squad!"

For a moment, I forget about the newspaper crumpled in my fist. Nothing helps my mental health like setting loose the dogs of war. This evening will be a triumph.

2.

"Time is not money. Money is a measurement of time, only one of multitudes of measurements. Time is infinitely more important than money. Money is nothing. Time spent on your students is everything. Do not let money sway, distract, or motivate you. Instead, keep yourself pure. Keep yourself clean."

The publication of an underground anarchist newspaper continues to consume my thoughts. It distracts me while I go about my duties. I cannot write in this state. I can hardly concentrate on the lockers.

As the Principal I take a personal interest in the contents of the school's lockers. They are property of the school before they are anything else. It is a privilege for the students to have private real estate for their own use. If the students choose to use the space allotted to them to store personal items, it's their choice. I must make sure that the students aren't choosing to abuse their privilege in ways that could be potentially harmful to fellow locker users. And that means both random and not-so-random locker searches.

The students are required to buy their lock from the school store and register their combination with the administration. Each lock also has a keyhole in the back. Naturally, I have a copy of the key.

Gary Dougan's locker is first, containing only books, clothes, and a bag of chips. The next one, Sarah Espenson's, is stuffed with notebooks, bags, make up, a nail file, and a mirror. Locker after locker fails to turn up any illegal materials, but they do provide some insight into the lives of my students. For example, I learn that Gary Hastert still has his Mom make his lunches and that Alicia Stone keeps a picture of her ex boyfriend taped next to her schedule. She really should move on.

My searching done, I rush to the opposite end of the campus. I have a meeting with my superior, Superintendent George Burnside. I try not to drop my guard as I hurry. Even this early in the semester, I must always be alert for the prevention of the senior prank. Not this year. Not this year. No live crickets released into the halls. No dressing the mascot in women's clothes. No sneaking obscene hand gestures during the class photo. Not this year.

"Adam! Great to see you!" Burnside says as I walk in.

Burnside is fifty years old, bald, dressed in a suit and wide tie. I can smell the alcohol vapors seeping from his skin. His cheeks are flushed. "How are you doing? I know the loss to Lincoln High can't have been easy for you."

"Oh, I'm keeping busy. Staying the course. Scheduling important meetings with faculty. Making sure Halloween decorations are up to code. Guiding the student council in their vital decisions. We have a school wide assembly coming up to raise awareness of community volunteering opportunities."

"Great, great. That's really all I needed to hear. I try not to tell you how to do your job. Just one thing, I noticed you haven't scheduled any time for standardized test preparation yet. I was wondering when you were thinking of getting started on that."

"George, I know you have an important job. You have politics to worry about. Palms to grease. Redistricting to oversee and back alley deals to make. You make sure the immensely complicated machinery that is a school district, a network of schools, can govern itself. You're higher on the totem pole than me, and you should focus your attention on top level stuff. Like long range curriculum plans. Let me worry about the day-to-day operations of the school. I've been doing this for eight years."

"I know, but part of my job is dealing with the... necessary bureaucracy that comes with a government position."

The part of your job that doesn't involve drinking, I add in my head. He isn't handling the fact that I take care of all the hard work well; it seems to make him feel like his job is just mindless goal-setting and political machinations. He probably thinks his job is the reason why he's unhappy. Not the large amounts of addictive depressant he consumes every day. Burnside needs to realize that taking pride in what you do not only makes life easier, it is the sole reason for living life. Justified pride, of course. I couldn't take pride in my work if I didn't do such a fine, thorough job. And if he can't enjoy his job, he should at least take solace in the high salary, however undeserved it may be.

"George, please, don't spend your valuable time worrying about it. The students will be prepared for the test. Remember when I instituted "fall break" just so you could use your timeshare on Lake Superior for a week? I didn't just do that to be popular- which I am- I did that so you could relax. You need to focus on the big picture, not sweat the little stuff."

I know what makes him relax, and my words have inspired him to take a pull from the bottle he keeps in his drawer. He slides down into his chair, comfortable now.

"Well, glad to hear you're not too distraught over football. As you said, don't sweat the small stuff."

I grit my teeth.

"Before you go, though, I was curious. Have you seen this?" Burnside holds up a copy of the Gazette. A new copy. The headline reads "CAFETERIA FOOD NOW FIFTY PERCENT REAL FOOD."

He continues, "It's funny. I think you've formed a very positive environment for these students, the kind that fosters creativity. It's nice to see them putting energy into something positive."

I keep breathing. I must show no emotion. Even though I eat the cafeteria food here every day. Not just to save money. I do it because I enjoy it. It's all I eat. I need to be sure that my students are having their nutritional needs more than met. I care so much for the health of my students, but I also want them to enjoy what I provide. So much of a school's reputation hinges on the quality of its food. I personally verify that each meal is delicious. I hand picked the chefs from a wide pool of qualified applicants. I serve gourmet meals, by any standard. How can I not take this libelous trash as a personal insult to everything I stand for? "I've seen it. I have to go."

I have to discover the identity of the insurgent reporters more than ever. It was easier to punish sedition in the old days: one just had to break the offenders' printing press. Now everyone has a printing press in their own house capable of shooting out pages with lightning speed. Not even I could destroy every one, as much as I would like to. I will need to choose my tactics carefully while dealing with this.

I make sure to wave at, greet, and laugh with every student I pass by on the way back to my office. Fourth period just ended and the students mob the hall. I can tell that everyone views me as being on their side; a teammate, representing them in a world that would rather toss them to the hungry wolves of cynicism and reality.

I'm scanning the crowd when my eyes lock with another's. They are emerald green and kind and I think I've never seen a more beautiful pair.

Then they're gone. My head whips around, trying to get a better look, but I can't tell to which retreating back the eyes belong. I feel like I've seen a ghost. I want to sell my soul for just one more look. But whoever she is, she's gone, and I still have an insurrection to suppress.

I'm about to go to the monitor room to see if the perpetrators have been caught on camera, when I'm distracted by a commotion. Outside, in the quad, I see a crowd of students in a clump. This is not the good kind of gathering, where students get together and discuss their happy lives. They're gathered in front of the bench where the student prayer youth group congregates. A good group of kids, dedicating their lives and sacrificing a little social standing in the name of something larger and more important than themselves. I can identify with that kind of thinking.

Up close, I can see that someone has carved "Jesus Wept" into the bench's wooden surface. "Why, Principal Kent?" asks Hannah Crest, a member of the prayer group. "Why would someone do this?"

I have a camera filming this area, but I don't need to check the footage to know who did this. Vandalism is a part of school life, such as the deep philosophical inquires found on bathroom walls. More serious vandalism, however, could only be committed by a few individuals that I know of. One in particular has issues with outspokenly religious students. "Don't worry Hannah. I'll punish this lawbreaker personally."

An hour later I am in my office, sitting behind a large polished mahogany desk. Lights are strategically placed to shine brightly on the chair in front of me while keeping myself in semidarkness. I am so glad I had it soundproofed. Besides the obvious benefits when I'm dealing with certain students, it makes the room totally silent. To me this makes thinking more enjoyable. Each thought can be savored.

I realize it's been over forty minutes since I called Brandon Nelson into my office. He should be stewing nicely by now. I call Ginny Wheeler, the office assistant, to send him in and she says yes and calls me by my first name. Lovely woman.

I need to clear my mind and prepare for the task at hand. Even though our loss to Lincoln High is burning a hole in my stomach and the new issue of the Gazette is causing my hands to wobble. The most pressing threat to the school's sanctity comes first.

Brandon saunters in. He's a short white teenager with the faintest beginnings of a mustache. He's wearing jeans that aren't quite pants or shorts, an expensive looking hooded sweatshirt and a Yankees baseball cap. He already has a sneer on his face.

I stand. "Hello Brandon. How are you? Take off your hat when you're indoors, please. It's disrespectful."

He sits down heavily and doesn't take off his hat. Having a student defy a direct order to my face makes my temples throb, but now is not the time to belabor the point.

I sit behind my desk and stop smiling to show him a hint of how much I disapprove of his existence. "I assume you're aware of the unfortunate event that occurred earlier today?"

"I assume you're wrong because I don't."

I stare at the hat still sitting crooked on his head, the brim obscuring part of his face. "Brandon, this is no joking matter. Apparently someone carved some hurtful words into the bench outside D-wing. As you can imagine, everyone is very upset. You know how popular those benches are for 'hanging out' between classes."

I pride myself on the use of popular vernacular. I've been trying to use that phrase in context all day. I hope I got it right. In any case, I now present him with the opportunity I know he won't take. "Brandon, do you know anything about what happened?"

"You can't prove anything, *sir*." As expected, he continues thinking he has all the power in this exchange. "I know nobody said I did it, because I didn't. So this is just you acting on a hunch and bringing me in because you hate me. And I wouldn't call those benches 'popular.' The only people who sat there are a bunch of fucking Jesus freaks, and that's *all* they did. Just sit there and moo about God."

And that reveals his motive. He cut up the bench because he didn't like the people who congregated around it. What a stupid reason to destroy school property. My property.

Time to prey on his weaknesses. First, I need to involve his parents. I know they are adults who give him everything he wants and who are somehow totally ignorant of his evil nature. Brandon needs this ignorance to justify his behavior more than anything else. It's good to show someone that their future relationships and economic streams are in immediate danger in order to bring them over to your way of thinking.

"Maybe I'm going about this the wrong way. How are your parents, Brandon? I see they're still buying you new hats. And a brand new car, too, now that you've got your license. You've got everything a boy could want. I don't understand why you behave like this towards others. What would your parents think?"

"I act like this towards others because they haven't earned my love," Brandon laughs, and actually stands up to leave. "The only evidence you have is a funny feeling. I know it and you know it. I gotta go to class now. Face it, this is the best thing that ever happened to those fags. They want to suffer- it brings them closer to God!"

This is going nowhere. This student still thinks he is in a position where he can leave without my permission. That's okay, I wasn't planning on appealing to Brandon's humanity or reason. I was planning on exploiting his insecurities. I reach into my pocket and throw a bag of marijuana onto my desk. "Sit down, please, or I call your parents and tell them about what I found in your locker."

Brandon's eyes turn into perfect circles. The day just got a little better. "You can't search my locker! You can't do that! You have no proof! It's against the law!"

Here we go. Time to educate a delinquent student on exactly what their position is in my school.

I grab his collar and pull his face so close to mine we almost kiss.

"I am the Principal! I am the law! I can do anything I want!" I explain, bugging my eyes and making the cords on the side of my neck stand out. I realize that his hat brim is rubbing my hair and messing it up.

"And take off your HAT!" I scream at him.

Brandon removes his cap. He stares at the floor, quivering and silent. I drop my hands and take a deep, cleansing breath. Relax. I sit back at my desk. Brandon still refuses to make eye contact. "Tonight you will ask your parents for three hundred dollars. Cash. And then you will give them to me. That should cover the cost of the bench. Tell them it's for a new hat."

Brandon blinks. "N-no! I can't do that! It's not right! I'll-"

"If you don't, I show your parents the marijuana and whatever sadomasochistic homosexual pornography I happen to have on hand. Who are they going to believe? They'll still love you, either way. But this way they won't have to find out about your vandalism."

Brandon sniffs. I can see him weighing the options in his head. I know he can only come up with one acceptable solution. "Okay," he whispers.

We sit in silence for a long time. He doesn't deserve my permission to leave, since he has so much disdain for direct orders. After a while he stands up awkwardly and shuffles to the door.

"Think about this the next time you decide to vandalize school property, " I say to him. Hopefully he will.

That didn't take too long. I check the clock: it's not even noon yet. In the soundproofed silence I feel my anger over the Gazette return, like feeling seeping back

12

into a numbed limb. One newsletter is a statement against my authority, but printing a second displays a hatred for this school that heats my blood. I need to identify those responsible. I need to use the cameras.

I walk from my office to the monitor room. The groups of students I pass all say "Hello, Mr. Kent" and wave. If the students all hate the cafeteria food, they don't show it. I hope they realize that someone who probably packs a lunch from home is threatening and ridiculing the delicious and free meals I provide as a service to the student community and staff. The Gazette is as serious a challenge to my rule as anything I have come across in my eight years at Bayview.

Inside the monitor room I rewind all the cameras to this morning. It's finally time for unblinking, omniscient information gathering. I have the entirety of the school covered, and as I watch students enter the school one by one to begin their day. I have each student's name committed to memory, and I assess relevant facts about each one, including how possible it is that they are the evildoers responsible for the Gazette. Maxine Grist, senior and important node of the string network: not likely. George King, sophomore and winner of the science fair? I don't think so. Each student I see is too involved in the school experience to strike against it with hurtful words. Yes, just words, but words used as a weapon cut just as deeply as any knife. Who is responsible for wounding me so much?

There.

In the corner of one screen I see a student place a stack of folded papers outside the E-Wing row of lockers. I can't make out his face, but I can tell he's wearing a standard issue sweater worn by members of the surfing club. He's limping slightly too. Only one member of the surfing club has been injured recently enough to still show signs: Jesse Corvall. Known associates include all members of the surf club, as well as his his best friend Tyler Durben. Then another male student, shorter than Jesse and wearing glasses, takes a paper off the stack and pins it to the bulletin board nearby.

Caught in the act of distribution. I know who my enemies are now, and while it doesn't cause their actions to hurt me any less deeply and personally, it does give me a sense of satisfaction. If they want to see this school crumble and fail, I need to stop them. I will show them the error of their ways, and give them a chance to repent for their sins. If they refuse, I will bring them to justice. The sanctity of this institution must be protected from assault at any cost.

"Nice to meet you, Jesse and Tyler," I whisper to the monitors.

3.

"Voting matters. As a Principal there are some laws you can't pass unilaterally. Democracy was invented for just this situation. You need to let the people decide. If you make your case well, not only will the changes you want to make be implemented but they will be accepted by the people well into the future- because they made the decision themselves. However, do not think that Democracy is entirely in the hands of others. Your vote counts too. If you are resourceful, you will make it count double."

One of my daily routines is inspecting the floor and desks of a vacated classroom for notes left behind by the students. It informs my picture of my students' social network and gives me a glimpse into their personal lives I wouldn't have otherwise. Sometimes I learn other important information.

This classroom recently held a freshman English class. I find a piece of paper folded into a triangle under a seat. I unfold it and read of an invitation to a lingerie party.

The hours are listed "10:00pm until sober enough to drive." This is disgusting. Freshmen shouldn't be thinking up such things in English class! They should be focusing on their gerunds and past participles. I see it's scheduled for tonight. I don't have much time. I grab the classroom phone and dial the phone number written on the back of the note.

"Hello?" a young girl giggles.

"Yes, this is Sergeant Griffith with the Bluff County Sheriff's office. I have a report of child endangerment on the premises of 1320 Washoe Lane. Apparently there are unsafe activities of a lascivious nature going on."

Silence. Then, "What do you mean?"

"Just letting you know that the police have been alerted. Increased patrols will naturally be occurring tonight, and the police will be coming by just to make sure nothing... unseemly is going on."

"N-nothing's happening tonight, officer. You must have the wrong number."

"Have a good day, ma'am. We'll be around."

I hang up. That should compromise their plans for the evening. Hopefully every freshman involved participates in some wholesome activity appropriate for their grade level instead, like a jigsaw puzzle or board game.

I remember when I came here eight years ago. The rolled-up maps on the walls were so old they still had the USSR. That was the first thing I changed. Then I fired all teachers who had been instructing students with the out of date maps. It wasn't my fault that they were lazy. The students always come first.

There's a flu going around. School is the perfect environment for the spread of contagion. Kept in the same close quarters as the infected, the number of healthy students that suddenly fall ill can increase exponentially over the course of a week. Not only are those students removed from the school system and its positive learning experience, but classes with a large number of conspicuously missing persons are much harder to teach and keep focused. If students see empty seats, it reminds them that they could be out sick too, but rather than being thankful that they are healthy, they envy those who get out of class! Sometimes a Principal's job can be thankless. However, I must continue to fulfill my duty.

Misty Lane fell ill today. I sent her to the nurses' office immediately, before she could spread the flu to the rest of the cheerleaders, or even worse, the football team. I scan the string network in my evidence room, tracing the string backwards from Misty's push pin. It helps to know who's kissing who when trying to stop a flu. I stop on Jake Masters' pin. Every pin connected to him has fallen sick. He must be the vector of this disease. If I quarantine him I can slow the spread and keep the flu from reaching critical mass. I pick out two other students who aren't sick yet but have been in contact with the infected. If I send these three to the nurses' office, the flu will be defeated

I leave the classroom and walk to Mr. Paba's Spanish class. I dread entering the room. Mr. Paba is the worst teacher I have on payroll at this school. He doesn't do anything that could get him fired, but neither does he do anything to help his students learn. As I enter, thirty students turn their dulled eyes toward me. It's a creepy sensation.

"The correct way to say it is 'Si se'... Yelena?" He looks at a Latino girl in the front row. Apparently he defers to native speakers when he's unsure of the answer. Maria yawns, and says "Si se puede."

"We've been working on the same sentence for twenty minutes," whispers Jake Masters. "Time has no meaning."

When the students are aware of each passing minute during class, the teacher is not doing their job. I try to make teachers as efficient as possible. I give them free coffee, and the closest parking spot I can provide. I even make sure to have at least one student familiar with audio visual equipment in each class, otherwise the teachers waste whole periods trying to get a video or powerpoint to play on the projector. With Mr. Paba, however, nothing seems to help. I wish I could save these students from their fate, but there's nothing I can do at the moment. Soon, I will have to have a talk with Mr. Paba.

"He assigns us all the problems in the book, straight busy work, and then he spends the whole period checking the price of gold online," Jake whispers again.

"You need to go to the nurse's office," I say. "You could be sick. I need to separate you from the healthy students."

"You mean... I'm free?" Twenty nine pairs of glazed eyes watch him stand up, and then look at the clock. I leave before I have to watch any more energy and spirit wither up and die due to lack of exertion. Danny looks like a man who just received a stay of execution.

"The air is so fresh," he says. "I thought I would be in that room forever."

Next, I trek to Mrs. Frank's History class. The students are in the midst of a discussion on Native Americans. I pull Carrie Lisbon outside.

"You need to go to the Nurse's office," I say.

"But I'm not sick," says Carrie.

"But you could be. You've come into contact with the infected. You could be a carrier. It's for the good of the school. Besides, you get out of class."

"But there's nothing wrong with me. I want to learn."

Of all the students who would kill to get out of class for the day, I have to quarantine the one who wants to stay.

"I'm sorry, but you pose a public health risk. I wouldn't do this unless it was absolutely necessary. You are currently a danger to others. The safety of my students is paramount. This sickness must be stopped now, or it will spread like wildfire and many days will pass before it takes its full course. Please, you must do this in the name of the greater good."

"So as an individual what I want is less important than what's good for the group?"

"As an individual in this school you must do what I tell you. You'll thank me later, when the sickness has passed." I lead her to the nurse's office, where she will wait until her parents pick her up. It was painful, but the crisis has been averted.

Like picking at a festering scab, my thoughts return to the Gazette. A new issue was disseminated today, the headline reading "PRINCIPAL KENT BLAMES LITTER ON LINCOLN-HIGH-BACKED SEPARATIST ORGANIZATION". Not only are they implying that there is a litter problem at this school, but they question my portrayal of Lincoln High as the ultimate enemy. Did the writers know that I spend every day fighting against litter, the inexorable force that will not stop? I personally put up posters against litter, hand pick the janitorial crew, and pick up the detritus that accumulates everywhere long after everyone else has left for the night. Making light of my crusade against litter, that's a low blow. The less seriously the students take the litter epidemic, the more they will discard their trash outside the designated receptacles, and the worse the problem will become. Tyler and Jesse have made this newsletter issue personal, and I must respond in kind.

But first, I must make an appearance at a Student Council meeting. Each of the ten members is elected by their peers, and is invested with an amount of power. While they don't have enough power to act on their own, since each official decision they make must be approved by me, they have enough to maintain the illusion that the Council can actually make important changes to the school. The illusion of power and representation is important to maintain; it keeps the machinery of the school running smoothly and without incident.

When I walk in, the students are discussing snack machines. "I think there should be a healthy option," says Erica Babst. "Right now they only vend sodas and candy."

What Erica doesn't realize is that healthy food doesn't sell. Students bring healthy food from home or eat the delicious and nutritious cafeteria food. The snack machines target those with extra cash in their pockets, and it's been proven that students like spending their extra income on foods that bring instant gratification. The income generated goes directly to the student council to spend on events, so it's really in their

15

best interest that the machines stay stocked with sugary snacks. It keeps the students coming back for more and redistributes money where it is needed most: the school.

"I'll take that into consideration, Erica," I say. I need to change the subject, so the healthy choices can be forgotten about. "By the way, what's student council's plans for homecoming dance decorations?"

Everyone speaks up at once, suggesting themes and styles for the dance. It takes thirty minutes for everyone to make their suggestions, and then ten more minutes to vote on a winner. I have final say, of course, but to keep the council happy I approve the winning theme: "Adventure on the High Seas". I congratulate the students for a productive and organized meeting and distribute snacks to the students as a reward for forgetting about healthy vending machine alternatives. I'm glad no one mentioned the Gazette in my presence.

New student council members are being elected today. Campaign posters cover the walls. One particular poster says "Tyler Dourdan for student council". Centered on the paper is a photo Tyler, smiling as if he's done nothing wrong.

So Tyler has aspirations of power, does he? I will need to oversee these elections carefully. The talent pool must be kept pure and free of any malignant presence like Tyler's.

"Make sure you store the ballots in this room in clearly labeled boxes for tallying. Post a guard." The council nods as they masticate.

I run quickly to the library and make my way behind the counter, nodding to Shelly the librarian. One of my first acts as Principal was to modify the software that logs and dates which books each student has checked out to include all the libraries in the city. Libraries that carry books I would never allow in my school. I enter Tyler's name, and look at the list that pops up. Lies My Teacher Told Me. The Biography of Thomas Paine. Revolutionary Fighters of Latin America.

This is all the evidence I need pertaining to the seriousness of Tyler's mental instability. He apparently harbors the delusion that what he is doing is somehow moral, somehow justified. Well, he could have expressed his journalistic proclivities at the official student newspaper. He could have had a noble, legal outlet for his writings. But he chose not to. Now, he must repent, he must take his one chance at forgiveness and salvation, or he will suffer the most dire consequences.

I stomp down the stairs and past the voting booths. I pat several voters on the back, congratulating them on fulfilling their civic duty and reminding them not to litter and that our cafeteria food is real food.

Tyler and Jesse have gym class together. I am pleased to see that they are wearing their standard issue gym uniforms as they play badminton; white logo'd shirt and black logo'd stretchy shorts. Everyone wears the uniform or they will be punished. The fourth period bell rings and the students begin to file into the locker room.

I stand in front of Tyler and Jesse, face to face at last.

I keep my breathing steady, relaxed, and cool. I casually lean my hand against the wall. "May I have a word with you two gentlemen?"

Jesse speaks first, in his surfer drawl. "I'd like to, but I have to get changed and get to math class. I have a test."

"And I have to vote for student council," says Tyler

"But you see, we have a fire drill scheduled, so we actually have plenty of time to chat."

I reach over and pull the fire alarm. The noise is almost painful as everyone else vacates the building. I stare at Tyler and Jesse until the ringing ceases.

They stare back. "There isn't a fire drill today."

I take a deep breath. "I just want to ask you: what's your excuse?"

"For what?" asks Jesse.

"For publishing a subversive, libelous piece of trash. For tainting the pure dispositions of my students with your lies. And for hurting my feelings."

Silence. Then Tyler speaks up. "They're just jokes. They're funny. It's nothing personal, we swear."

"Good to hear, Tyler. I'm glad you've admitted to authorship, that's very important for everyone involved. Now that's out of the way, all you have to do is apologize. And agree to stop publishing the Gazette."

"We won't do that," says Jesse. "What we're doing isn't against the law."

"I am the Principal. I am the law in this school."

Tyler pushes up his glasses. "But this is America. Freedom of press is in the Constitution."

"This is not America. This is Bayview High. If you continue this sedition, you will pay the ultimate price."

"It's nothing personal, but it's too funny to give up right now. Thanks for your concern, Principal Kent." They walk away smiling.

Well, I tried to let them take the easy way out. I clench and unclench my hands in anticipation of the work ahead.

The entire student body has followed the evacuation plan perfectly and are calmly assembled in the parking lot and football field. I am so proud of them.

Chris Hasty, my loyal Vice Principal, is waiting for me on the field. "Why did someone have to pull the fire alarm? I hate talking to firefighters," he groans.

"Hopefully it was pulled for the greater good."

"Adam, we need to go over the budget, alright? The school is still a little short for the month, even counting the private donations."

I imagine how good Jesse must feel, now that he knows how much the Gazette offended me. "I'll definitely go over it with you soon, Chris. I'm busy with student council business unfortunately. For now, cut all funding to the surfing club. Surfboard wax is expensive, and allowing them out of class for competitions is against policy."

I put one arm around Chris. "Things to do. Remember to vote. Goodbye."

I tread as fast as I can to the student council room. Mary Ellen, junior, is standing guard outside the door.

"Fire drill, Mary," I say. "Go congregate with your fellow council members. I'll watch the ballots. Fire hazard, you know." Mary sneezes before she leaves. Oh no. Another disease vector? "Go to the nurse's office instead please! That sounds like a cold. Please separate yourself from all other people!"

I need to hurry before the council returns from the fire drill. The first box of ballots lies untaped at my feet. A stack of blank ballots lies on the table. I pull out a pen, and check the box next to Tyler's rival candidate on one ballot after another after another. Each one lowering Tyler's chances a percent or more. Voter turnout has been poor lately.

Each time I fake a signature of a student I know to be too lazy or distracted to vote, I hear Tyler telling me the Gazette is just too funny to give up right now.

I check another box. Well Tyler, I find this funny. We just have different senses of humor. I'm so busy with the school, I don't laugh as much as I should. It's hard to inspire a school rivalry week after week. It's hard to sell ad space at football games, provide free and reduced lunches, keep history books up to date, punish vandalism, and fight litter. It's hard to mediate interdepartmental conflicts, hire math teachers who are actually certified in mathematics, and calm down angry parents. It's so hard to be the Principal I don't laugh as much as I should. So I laugh now and check another box.

I love Democracy.

4.

"Some students are lost causes. Lost causes are disobedient children impossible to mold into future positive members of society. They are broken beyond repair. However broken does not mean useless."

The man across from my desk is named Barry Green. He is young and eager and flexes his fingers despite himself. His shirt and slacks are clean. His tie is straight. He is, at first examination, completely inoffensive and non threatening. He thinks he wants to work here, I can tell. As the Principal, I must determine whether he actually wants to be here. I must strip him down to his barest desires, and see whether teaching is one of them.

"Barry, good to finally meet you in person."

"Same here, sir. I'd just like to say that I really want to work here."

"Great. I'll keep this very informal and just ask you a few questions pertinent to the hiring process."

"Anything you'd like to know, sir. Anything."

"What kind of experience do you bring to the table?"

"I worked as a substitute at Branciforte middle school for two years, then Stevenson Elementary for two, and I got my credential and my master's at BSU.

"And why do you want to teach here?"

"The location is beautiful. The teachers all love it here. But really, I just want to help kids learn and succeed in life."

"Good, great." I monitor his respiration rate, check his temples for sweat. I inspect his eyes for jitters before speaking again. "What kind of student were you in college?"

"My freshman year I wasn't very focused on my schooling, you know how it is, with the girls and the drinking..."

I make a chuckling sound in my throat.

"But after that I got excellent grades. I finished with a 3.8."

"Do any drugs?"

He looks slightly taken aback. "Not since freshman year, sir."

"Would you provide a urine sample?"

"Right now?"

"Would you?"

"Sure, I guess."

Slight perspiration about the hairline. He's nervous, but not lying, yet. "Did you ever cheat in school?"

"When I was younger, but not in college-"

"Ever cheat on a girlfriend?"

"I don't think that's relevant."

"If you want to get hired it is."

"Once."

"Were you ever in a war?"

"I never served in the military"

I reach into my jacket pocket and pull out a yearbook photo of Cassandra Day, freshman. "How old is this girl?"

"Not old at all. Extremely young, actually."

"Don't get smart. How old is she? Accuracy matters to me."

"Fifteen."

"Good guess. Are you a sex offender?"

"No!"

"You're pretty good at guessing a minor's age for a non-offender."

"I'm a teacher!"

"How do you feel about minorities?"

"How do I... I like them the same as anyone else, I suppose."

"Really? You'd treat a minority exactly the same as a white person? Exactly?"

"Is that bad?"

I scrutinize the size of his pupils and count his pulse by watching his throbbing temple. "So you wouldn't give an African American person preferential treatment?"

"No, I wouldn't."

"Even after your people oppressed him for four hundred years?"

"I... it wasn't my 'people' who did that."

"Yes it was, gringo."

"But I didn't do that. I believe in equality!"

"Equality means something else to those who got a four hundred year head start." Barry's hand leaves wet streaks on the table as he drags them to his forehead.

"Have you ever masturbated to pornography featuring one or more 18 year olds?"

"I can't say. You'd have to ask the producers."

"If a gunman entered your classroom, what would you do?"

"Call the cops."

"No time."

"Get security."

"No time."

"I- I confront him."

"How?"

"I tell him... to leave?"

I let that statement lay in front of us like a gutted fish. Barry senses my displeasure. "I order him to leave."

"You throw yourself in front of the gun. You fight him until he kills you. That's the only way the children have time to escape."

"That doesn't sound right."

"Are you saying that if such a situation presented itself you would be unwilling to make the ultimate sacrifice for your students?"

"No!"

"In this school, your life is forfeit. Your students' safety is your only concern."

"Okay."

"Would you commit murder to protect your students?"

"Yes." No hesitation this time. A fast learner.

"One last question." Barry nods, tense and ready. If I told him to fill a cup right here in my office he would. "You're playing Monopoly with your grandson for the first time. Do you let him win?"

"Uh, no I don't. If I let him win, he won't try as hard. He needs to learn that Monopoly takes skill and experience, the sooner the better."

"Even if he gets so frustrated he cries and tells his parents that you molested him?"

"He won't do that."

"Allegations of sexual indiscretions are a reality of public education. I have a clean school. I have a safe school. I won't have its good name tarnished by a sexual scandal, be it based on a false accusation or not."

"So I should let him win, and compromise my principals?"

"If you allow him to win without him knowing it, you gain the moral high ground. In time, he will be allowed to taste the sharp, bitter sting of defeat.

"So, do you still want the job?"

"Yes. Even more now. You must think I'm not cut out to be a teacher here. I will prove you wrong."

"Come back next week. In the meantime, practice techniques for disarming an armed individual with your bare hands." We shake. I will test him further next week. He bumps into my VP, Chris Hasty on the way out.

A man in his late twenties follows behind Chris. He has a receding hairline and a small ponytail. His beard exists mostly in his neck area, and he has on a T-shirt that says "There's no place like 127.0.0.1".

"Hello Chris, and hello Mr...."

"Lorence Anderton. I work for you."

"Of course! If not sure if I remember what you do, however."

Chris speaks up. "I hired Lorence to help run the school's servers, website and computer lab."

"You can call me the IT guy, though. It's shorter."

"Nice to formally meet you. What seems to be the matter?"

Lorence strokes his neckbeard. "Someone is using a teacher's account to input students' official grades in the system. From there the grades go direct to the transcript printer."

"That doesn't sound like a problem. Sounds like the system is working properly. Much easier than recording everything by hand."

Chris again: "This is a unique case, Adam. The teacher in question is Stuart Mills, and he's been out sick the last two days."

Lorence nods. "Last time I checked they were still logged into the server from somewhere on campus. They've been on for two hours, at least."

"I see." I take some time to digest the information. While this user is definitely in violation of the rules, and utilizing privileges and powers they shouldn't, they are not directly challenging my authority. Rather, they are defying their teacher's authority to assess what kind of student they are. Their actions indicate bravery, creative thinking, and above-average intelligence and familiarity with technology. However, they are also sullying the sanctity of the grading system. There are very few things I hold more sacred. Everyone is capable of getting A's in any of my classes. If you don't do well, you're not trying hard enough. You don't become a bad student after years of bad grades. You were a bad student before you got the grades; the letter just reflects the objective, inarguable reality of the situation. High-grade students are like high-grade meat at the grocery store: top quality, peak desirability, and high value. I try to maintain a high concentration of high grade students at this school. The undesirable, unpredictable and low value students are kept sectioned off in the lower tracks, and their numbers are thinned through expulsions and failing grades like hunters thin the deer population. Only those who want to put effort into their education deserve the privilege of staying in Bayview.

The question now becomes: is this student putting effort into their education? They are technically working within the system. If they get good grades by cheating, they're playing the system against itself, and deserve their grades. If I catch them, however....

I try to think of which of Mr. Mills' students have the skills necessary to pull off a heist of this caliber and the grades that mandate cheating as the only viable option. None come to mind. This opportunist's location must be found, then. They must be caught in the act before they escape or they will have committed the perfect crime.

"Do you know what computer this person is using?"

"Not the exact location, just that he's somewhere in this school. The network can't be accessed through a remote connection."

"Good to know. Chris, you search the computer lab. Lorence, you check the library. I'll check Stuart's classroom." We separate. I take the shortest possible path past the B-wing lockers and the west gym. As I walk past the woodshop my nose fills with the scent of sawdust. The choir room emanates the angelic sound of the Advanced Class. It feels like being in the presence of the divine.

Stuart has no class fourth period so the room should be empty. I peek in through the window and see a girl behind Mills' computer. She wears a white ruffled blouse and has pearl earrings peeking behind her dark curls. I recognize her: Melissa Pinkerton, senior, and Stuart Mills' trusted TA. I silently open the door and creep inside.

"You wouldn't happen to be using your teacher's admin code to change your classmates' grades, are you?" Melissa jumps like she just touched a live wire.

"Honesty counts a lot in my book," I add.

She sighs, quietly and quickly accepting her fate. "Yes I am."

"How did you do this? Is the system broken?"

"No. Mr. Mills lets me enter his grades all the time. He gave me his password. I used a few hacks, but they won't permanently damage the system. God, I feel really bad about this. He trusted me!"

"I bet you didn't feel bad about it a minute ago. But your grades are excellent. You didn't need to do this."

She's calmer than I expected. "I want the power to change my friends' lives."

I understand that desire. It's what drove me to become the Principal. If I didn't catch her she would have had true power. I've found that true power is invisible to those controlled by it.

"I'll tell you how this is going to play out. You will be suspended. You will not walk with the other graduates this summer. And Berkeley will most likely revoke your admission."

Her face falls steeply. "I'm not getting into college? But my parents, my friends... I'll miss out on everything! Oh my God, I can't even think of what this will do to my life!"

"Do you have a second choice school?"

"Yes. UC Santa Cruz."

"Well, the good news is that UCSC will happily admit you."

She doesn't believe it. She just stays silent, thinking I'm making fun of her.

"Really. Young people who know how to master technology, hackers specifically, are in giant demand. Plus, this shows that you take the initiative in your life. They'll probably hire you through work-study to help them run their servers too."

"So you're not going to ruin my life?"

"No. In fact, if you undo all the changes you've made, we can both pretend like you hacked your way in from scratch. Mills never needs to know you betrayed his trust."

"Thank you. And thanks for not yelling at me, Principal Kent."

"You're a good student. Maybe a little too ambitious, but good. I'm just curious though: did you just improve your friends' grades, or did you lower your enemies' grades too?"

She looks down at the floor. I sense shame. "I lowered grades too."

She's had a taste of true power, and used it to do both good and bad. I wish I could continue to watch her after she leaves this school, to see which path she ultimately chooses. There's only so much I can do, and beyond that it's just intention and the ability to resist temptation. I call in Chris Hasty, who leads her to the reception area. I have to prepare to talk to her parents.

I try working on The Principal's Guide to Success but my writing room is now the monitor room and it's nearly impossible to write with all those screens gleaming in front of me. I've grown very fond of watching all the various live feeds from the security cameras simultaneously. I could stare all day, and then at night re-watch what's recorded so I can catch everything I missed. It didn't take everyone long at all to forget about the cameras. Now they act like no one's looking. Meanwhile, I study behavior patterns. Traffic flow. I get to see the fruits of my labor enjoying their pristine natural environment. It's like watching the the movements of a well crafted watch. The coffee in the teacher's lounge is strong and passing right through me. I need some water.

Bayview High's drinking fountains are the uncontested best. They are at the perfect height and made of unblemished stainless metal. The handles move with the slightest application of force. The nozzle is expertly engineered. The jet of water is strong and fast but not overwhelming, providing just the right amount of water in each sip. The icy cold water is delightfully crisp with no coppery aftertaste. Each time I take a drink I feel delight that my students also experience the same joy. I am also pleased that students in other schools must feel acute dissatisfaction with their drinking experience. As I turn around and wipe my lips, a female student walks in my direction.

All my motion stops dead.

The sight of her hits me like a hammer but cuts like a machete. Her hair is dark but glossy with soft waves like a calm ocean and cut to a perfect length. Smooth, shapely legs. Her eyes are the green of deep, clean, sunlit water. Her skin the color of creamed and stirred coffee. She walks gracefully and with the energy of youth. I find her beauty to be unparalleled and unbelievable.

I should say something to her. I desperately want information about her, about her life. I want to know why she's so engrossing to me, why I suddenly have tunnel vision, why she makes my palms sweaty and my breath short. I should talk to her. Give her subtle hints about my feelings. Make her laugh. The options are limitless.

Now she's close, and I have nothing. My mind blanks like a tibetan monk deep in meditation. All I can do is stand there with my mouth open, struck dumb and empty-headed.

She smiles at me and the world justifies its existence. Her hand lifts, and just the fingers wave quickly in sequence. I wave back, utterly silent. I can't help but turn after she passes. Her hips sway in unison with her buttocks, which are wrapped tightly in a peach skirt. They could stop an army in its tracks. They could end wars. And then they pass away.

I catch my breath. I never feel attracted to students. Not that they're not attractive. I can proudly say my students are hotter on average than Lincoln High's by far. I protect them, care for them, and guide them through life, but I'm not close to them. I'm not their friend. My job requires that I keep an appropriate distance and not be involved in their lives outside of school. I must treat each student equally and fairly, and not show preference. That would indicate fallibility.

So why does it feel like I just ran a mile in record time? Why is a ten second silent encounter enough to make me unsteady for the rest of the day? Why do I stand here, still thinking about her?

I thought I knew every student on sight and by name. But not her. It's possible I'll never know who she was or see her again. This is the kind of cold reality I'm trying to shield my students from. May they never feel this pain.

The sound of basketball shoes squeaking. A young boy walks into view. I can identify Brandon Nelson at a long distance. No one else wears high end clothing so indifferently. He sees me, too, and a scowl appears on his face.

"Hey Mr. K. Invade anyone's privacy today? Read the new issue of the Gazette?"

The Gazette. Could he be involved in it's production too? Doubtful. He doesn't know Tyler and Jesse and isn't refined enough to disobey me beyond name calling and vandalism. Still, just in case he's involved I need to show him I'm not to be trifled with. I check all around me. There are scattered groups of students, all talking and oblivious to Brandon and I.

I yank him into a spacious, empty supply closet and close the door.

"What the fuck?" Brandon sputters.

I push him lightly but firmly against the wall.

"Don't fucking touch me!" he yells. No one outside can hear him, though. The door is thick. I pat him down quickly, avoiding the inner thighs.

"No!"

But it's too late. I feel the bulge in the pocket of his designer jeans and pull out a small baggie half full of white powder.

I'm not angry at Brandon yet. I'm just shocked by the hardness of the drug and also the sharp, primal urges I feel towards the substance. Not too long ago I'd double barrel it all without thinking twice. It's not a lot, but my tolerance is so low now. It'd be just what I need after a long day at school. A little pick me up....

I open the bag and get some residue on my index finger, then suck on it. Tastes like quality cocaine, cut with bleached flour.

"Are you a drug dealer? Are you selling this poison to my students?"

"I'm not selling it. It's just for me."

"Do you have any idea what it would be like managing a school full of cokeheads? Huh? All jumpy and paranoid, only caring about their next hit? You would do this to me?"

"I'm not selling it! I've never even done it before! Let me out of here!"

"I should expel you for this. But that's what you want, isn't it? Tell your family I'm the bad guy, then enroll in Lincoln High before the dust settles and reveal all my secrets to them? Your kind fits in well there. You'd be right at home among the lowlifes."

Brandon just glares and holds himself like he's expecting a punch to the mouth.

"Where'd you get this from?"

"Jack Hadley told me to hold it for him. I was going to give it back!"

"Well, it's mine now. I will search your locker every day. I may even do random pat downs. And if I ever find you with drugs again, or even hear whispers of you selling drugs, I'll expel you. But first, I'll break your knee. You'll never walk without limping ever again. Sound good?"

"You wouldn't."

"I think of myself as a patient person. I will tolerate you like I tolerate a mosquito buzzing around my head. But as soon as you land, overstep your bounds and try to take a bite-"

I clap my hands in front of Brandon's face. He flinches.

"Do. Not. Test. Me."

He pushes me away, and I let him run out the door. I know he won't complain to anyone. He'll sullenly harbor a grudge. He'll either change soon, let go of his anger and actually become a decent, contributing member of my school, or he'll crack and totally lose it. It's risky, keeping him here. But I can't let him win. That will prove there are youths out there I can't control. And if he reforms, it will be a great victory for me. I'm not one to give up.

Still, I will watch him like vultures watch the dying.

I want to watch the camera feeds for a while before school ends, but on my way to the monitor room I feel someone tap me on the shoulder. Ivan Novak, English Lit teacher, blinks at me. "Adam, I really need to talk to you. It's urgent. I don't know who else to go to."

"Of course, Ivan. Please, come into my office."

When we get there he lands in the padded chair like a sack of cement.

"You look like you've got a lot on your mind."

"I need to talk to you about... something. But you have to promise that you won't fire me."

"I promise. Everything we talk about in here in confidential. Plus, you're a good teacher. You're a good man. Now tell me what's wrong."

The light reflects off his balding head. "It's the thongs."

I can't determine what he means by this. "The footwear?"

"No, the underwear."

"What about the underwear?"

"You know what I'm talking about, though?"

"Yes, I am aware of the current fashion trend." In reality, I am not. I am too focused on being the best Principal in the world to worry about fashion or culture or who the President is.

"Some of my students, when they're sitting down or bending over, some of it shows."

"I see."

"There's different styles, you know? There's the kind with the little triangle, there's the thicker, v-shaped kind, and there's the kind that's just perpendicular strips. That's the worst."

"Worst?"

"When I see the underwear- and I can't help but look, they're peeping out all the time- I can't look away. I'm scared they'll see me staring, but I just can't help it. I-I mean-" he stammers, "they must want me to see it. They only wear it because they know it distracts me."

"I don't think they're wearing them for you..."

"They know how provocative it is to show a little thong. It makes me wonder what the whole thing looks like. Makes me picture what they look like putting it on, taking it off. What it would feel like pulling it back and snapping it, right? Then I start to wonder who else in the class is wearing one. Who the good girls are, who the naughty ones are. If any of the boys here have seen them, the whole thing. It's all a game to these girls, like some perverted morality test. I mean, what else can I think? What kind of girl is willing to wear such a thing, just to give me a brief glimpse? The less I see of it, the more is left to my imagination. Why are they doing this to me?"

"You have to realize it's not about you. It's all about them exploring their sexuality. They're not doing it to provoke you."

"But it does! You know what I'm talking about! Don't tell me you've never seen them, some of the older ones, flashing a little bit of G-string. If they weren't wearing any underwear at all, I wouldn't even care. But the fact that they deliberately wear it... it means they're willing to do anything in bed. Anything you want."

"This is unhealthy thinking. You can't see such things as temptations; they're not. Underwear choice doesn't imply anything about a person, it's just how they choose to express themselves."

"Just expressing themselves, hah! You don't understand, the underwear goes so far up in their area you wouldn't be able to see it below their gluteal cleft. It draws your eyes straight down, right to the goods. They're offering it, presenting it to whoever's looking. I just want to spank them. Pull down the pants, just the pants- so I can see the thong- and just spank their ass. Not hard, just enough to make it jiggle. Just enough to let them know I'm in charge."

"Will you act on these feelings?"

He looks shocked. "Of course not! I'm a professional! I'm married, happily! It's just... It's not right, flaunting themselves like that. It can't be comfortable. I've started wearing them myself, just so I can get a better idea of what it looks like. Not comfortable at all."

I wonder if wearing girl's underwear is the symptom of some psychological condition. Ivan interprets my silence as permission to continue free-associating. "You know they get pierced down there, too?"

"I doubt very much that anyone in this school has their clitoris pierced. You have to be an adult to get a piercing like that. Maybe girls at this school aren't completely naive about such matters but none of them are going to do something like that. They'll at least wait until college."

Ivan nods. His unfocused eyes indicate that he's not listening. "I'm thinking of getting one."

"You... you don't have a clitoris."

"No, the guy kind. The head of the penis. I read that women really like it when it's pierced like that. It hits the right spot."

This is rapidly becoming too disturbing. When it comes to my students I want to know about their personal lives, what makes them tick, their hopes, dreams and fears. I want to know everything about them. Everything I learn helps me serve them better. And everything I learn about them is rewarding and justifies more digging. My teachers, on the other hand....

Sometimes you can learn too much about someone.

"I appreciate you bringing this to my attention. Unfortunately, I cannot force girls to stop wearing thong underwear any more than I can force you to stop noticing them. All I can say is that you should be strong. What's my number one rule that I tell all my teachers?"

"No touching," Ivan says. He looks depressed.

"That's right. No touching. If it helps, maybe you could wear the underwear during school yourself. If you flash the girls a little thong, it might make the whole thing uncool. Just think about it."

We shake, and he leaves my office to continue his fruitless obsession. Sometimes it's reassuring to know I'm the only adult in this school qualified to be Principal. Sometimes it isn't.

5.
"Halloween is a perfect opportunity for appropriate personal expression. It is also a perfect opportunity for inappropriate personal expression. Censor with abandon."

I'm in the east wing bathroom washing my hands and scrutinizing my outfit in the mirror. It's a good thing I keep extremely fit. If I wasn't running the track and lifting weights every day after school ended the blue latex would not be nearly as flattering on me like it is now. The red cape is a little short, but that's better than having a dirty cape dragging on the ground behind you all day, getting caught on things. The S on my chest is a brilliant crimson. The students and faculty won't understand the costume. They'll like it, especially the women (due to the tightness), but they won't understand why I choose to be Superman for Halloween. It's not because I want to be Superman. It's because I happen to have Superman's job.

Understand, I don't think I'm a superhero. Far from it. I'm just an ordinary man. But Superman and I share the burden of being responsible for the safety of a large number of people. He has to protect the people of Metropolis from aliens, mad scientists, and monsters, and I have to protect the people of Bayview High from psychopaths, rapists, drug dealers, gangs, rabid animals, and marauding bands of Lincoln High loyalists. There's only one difference in how Superman and I do our jobs: Superman gets to wear a garish, easily recognizable costume and be adored by the masses after every battle. Me? I get a paycheck. I wear a suit. No one thanks me to my face for saving children's lives every day. I am invisible to most, even when I'm doing my most important work or making my most important plans. For example, no one noticed me promote the three previous gym teachers to history teachers, and then from history teachers to administration positions. It just seemed like business as usual. Except now, there is no one else in Bayview who can check my power. The Vice Principal focuses entirely on his job, and the other administrators are indebted to me for promoting them so fast. They'd never be foolish enough to meddle in my affairs, which frees me up to make more plans. That'd be my superpower, if I had one.

Invisibility.

I admire the effort the students put into their costumes. I would never institute a policy requiring student uniforms since young people need a way to express themselves through dress. Students need that freedom. Still, I always need to look for those few students who choose an inappropriate costume. Halloween is not about being inappropriate or gruesome, it's about expressing dark ideas in a healthy way while contributing to school spirit. It's fine to be scary, but not at the cost of other students' delicate complexions. I smile and compliment every costumed student I see.

"Nice werewolf," I tell Kyle Christianson.

"What a great nurse," I say to Kayla Espers.

"Wonderful gh-" I stop. Someone is wearing a sheet over their body with holes cut out for eyes. "Tell me your name, right now."

"I'm Eric Chan. What the problem?"

"Take that costume off, right now."

"What? Why?"

"It's racist. That sheet is far too pointy at the top. Take it off."

"I'm not dressing like the KKK! I'm a ghost! It's just a sheet!"

I lean in close to where I think his ear is. "If you don't take off right now I might twist it up and hang you by your ankles with it."

He takes it off. "Next time find a sheet that's less pointy," I say. "There's some face paint in the teacher's lounge. Be a skull, that's much cooler than a ghost." I can't abide even the hint of racism. I slick back my hair again and continue through the waves of students, my red boots tapping on the tile.

My foot slips, and before I look down I know what I've stepped on. It's the Gazette. The headline reads "PRINCIPAL CUTS FUNDING TO CLUBS, SPENDS PROFIT ON HOOKERS."

Suddenly my suit is too tight and too hot. My molars grind against each other involuntarily. It's so profane. So base. There's no creativity in it, just a cheap ploy for easy laughs. I thought cutting off the surfing club would stop Tyler and Jesse, but it's just made them more prolific and more enraged. This is the second Gazette this week, and they're not attacking the school anymore. They're attacking me personally, each time. A cunning plan must be hatched, one that will solve this problem once and for all.

And no half measures. Whenever I find graffiti, I don't tell the janitors to paint over the letters. Even if they used the same color paint, the area covered over would still stand out. Instead, I tell them to repaint the whole wall. That way, it's like the graffiti never existed. That's what I have to do to Jesse and Tyler. I need to paint the whole wall.

Gary Gaspar and Marian Lee, seniors, walk by. The timing is excellent, as my vision was beginning to dim from anger. Just seeing them calms me. The former is dressed in overalls, a red shirt and a red hat with a fake mustache and plunger. Marian wears a pink dress and blonde wig. I greet them warmly and comment on how wonderful their costumes are.

Every high school has its "golden couple",: the kind of people who are unsurpassed in their popularity and yet still decent, smart, and caring. It's rare enough to have one such person in a school; for many years the most socially gifted students at this school were a coven of letterman-jacket-clad sociopaths who I later caught hazing new football teammates by forcing them to swim in the freezing ocean at night wearing nothing but garter belts, athletic supporters and lace bras. It's even rarer for a Principal to be gifted with two such people, and to have them fall in love with each other. I admire their restraint in how often they show each other affection in the halls and, naturally, on camera, or else the jealousy they inspire could have a disastrous effect on anyone who walks near. It doesn't matter how jealous one is of them, though, one never gets mad at them. That's why they're the golden couple.

I've had two golden couples in my eight years at Bayview High. One of the most important aspects of my job is keeping golden couples alive. I don't know what it is, but two young perfect people in love are extremely susceptible to tragic accidents their senior year of high school. Something about life being so good and the future so bright, combined with the building fear that something as wonderful and enriching as high school is about to end once and for all... it makes one a little reckless.

"Remember, Gary," I tell the garishly dressed plumber, "drive carefully around sharp turns tonight, especially the Ash Street intersection. If a trick-or-treater steps in front of you, don't swerve. You could crash and die. Trick or treaters are like deer, they'll jump out of the way."

"Okay Mr. Kent, I'll be extra careful tonight," says Gary, and grins.

I clap them both on the back and make my way to the next room. I wasn't going to stop by Mrs. Relstab's driver's education class, but Gary and Marian have reminded me about the attention I focus on inspiring safe driving in my students. Specifically, I make sure that the driver's education class saves the "Red Asphalt" screening for Halloween.

The room I enter is dark, except for the blue glow of the TV and the hum of the ancient VHS player. Witches, pro athletes, movie stars, monsters, and animals stare at the screen, their eyes wide. They've heard of the video from their friends, but now they actually get to see it. It's my opinion that they *need* to see it.

Teenagers need to learn to be careful around cars, and to not tempt fate by mixing cars with drugs, alcohol, or simple recklessness. And if seeing a steering wheel embedded and stuck deep into someone's forehead, or flappy chunks of brain scooped up off the pavement, or a stream of blood pouring from an opened door keeps just one person from making a fatal mistake one night, my work here is done.

Mostly I keep my eyes closed, and listen to the ghouls' and goblins' gasps and yelps and cries. One girl keeps sobbing in random gulping breaths; I can tell it's Ashlee Simmons by the sound.

Now's the part with the kid whose face falls half off. The sounds are graphic.

After it's all over, I say, "Have a safe Halloween! Be sure to dodge any errant drivers! Remember to jump to the side if you can't get behind cover!" The class is silent. Indeed, my work here is done.

My cape sways in the breeze as I amble. I like the feeling. Chris Hasty, my vice principal, is dressed as a Jenga tower. It goes well with his tie. He walks alongside me when he sees I won't stop striding past him. He says something, but I don't listen to what he says, I just nod. Something about money, of course. I scan the gym as I sweep past, hoping to catch sight of Tyler or Jesse, the "journalists." I see the class is playing a variant of dodgeball, called prisonball.

"You know what I like about prisonball?" I ask Chris.

"Uh, what? The dodging?"

"Yes, but more specifically what the dodging accomplishes. You see in this game, once you're out, you go to prison, located behind the remaining players. If you catch a ball in prison, you can throw them at others and try to get them out. The game prepares them."

"For what?"

"Well, wearing uniforms, for one thing. But it also prepares them for everyday life. Let's say you're tick or treating near the Ash Street intersection when somebody comes around the corner behind you, tires screeching. Your prisonball instincts kick in. You take a quick look, accurately determine the threat, and then jump out of the way. Threat from the rear successfully dodged."

"That's true. What a great game! Anyway, I'm glad you agree with me that we should start drumming up support for the proposition now. I think if we start working the phones constantly, raising as much awareness as we can, we'll be able to reappropriate some of the property tax money...."

I tune him out again. I do so much good for this community, save so many lives from death by vehicle. Why do the dissatisfied troublemakers have to be the most vocal? I will confront Tyler one more time, he's obviously the weaker of the two. If I can break the two boys apart, separate them from one another, the Gazette will fail.

"Also, Mr. Paba's locked in his closet. Just thought I'd let you know."

"What?" Just as I had feared. Mr. Paba's incompetence has inspired mob rule. There is a vacuum where there was once a position of authority, albeit a weak and fat position.

"Nothing big. I guess he unlocked it to get something, left the keys in the door, and the wind pushed it shut. I've got the janitor on the way, he just needs to finish fixing the heating duct in my office."

"The wind. Right. No, I think this is something big indeed. The rule of law has been suspended. I must bring it back. Anarchy will not win, the paper will not win. Not today."

I run to the office as fast as I can, cape fluttering. I reach under my desk and pull out the axe I keep hidden there at all times. It's a fireman-style axe, with a long sharp point opposite the blade. I run back through the empty halls into Mr. Paba's class.

The students don't notice me. They're talking with one another, relaxed, and happy. But they have not earned this happiness. They have taken it by force, by locking in their teacher.

"Who has the keys?" I yell.

Everyone goes quiet, but no one answers.

I heft the axe in one hand. "Last chance. Anyone?"

A zombie in a suit says, "What's the axe for?"

Chris the Jenga tower walks in. "Oh! Mr. Kent, like I said, the janitor's on his way. You can put the axe down."

"No time. The school year is only a certain number of minutes. The period is almost half over! The students must be educated, even on Halloween!" I swing the axe into the closet door. Mr. Paba screams. I swing the axe again. Some students start screaming.

"Adam, please stop!" yells Chris. Thunk!

"Please!" Thunk!

I wipe the sweat slick bangs from my forehead. "It's just a door, Chris." This is why not everyone can be Principal. Principals need to make the tough decisions.

"Oh Jesus, Jesus Christ..." blubbers Mr. Paba.

Thunk! Thunk! Thunk! The students have stopped screaming. "Seriously Adam, I'll have the door unlocked in a minute," mutters Chris.

"Hang in there Raymond! Almost... done!" I give the door a good kick and the center splinters apart. Mr. Paba blinks in the light, sobbing.

He's wearing a Superman costume. Who does he think he is? I'm Superman! I clutch the axe tightly.

I made sure to have my secretary put in the staff bulletin that I was going to be Superman for Halloween. I mean, if a student did it, I wouldn't care. They can dress as whomever they want. But I expect respect from my staff. Or at least some semblance of dignity.

"For God's sake, Raymond. You could have at least been Batman." Tight blue spandex does not look good stretched over his round body. Not like it does on me. I lean back and continue to front-kick the remains of the door, pieces of which fly everywhere. "Stop crying!" I yell.

Scooter the janitor walks into the class, dressed in coveralls and a Dodgers cap. "Got the key..." he trails off.

I snatch it from him. "Thanks, this is totally necessary now," I mutter. I unlock the doorknob, and the small chunk of door it's attached to falls to the ground. "Clean this up, Scooter. And you can come out now," I tell Mr. Paba. His nose drips snot while he squeezes out of the closet.

He gulps. "I... that axe was so close to my head-"

"Now's not the time. You have thirty minutes left in class and forty minutes' worth of Español to enunciate. Chop chop!"

"I can't, I can't teach now. I was in fear for my life! I need to go home, I need to rest and recover."

"That's a lie, you were completely safe! Do you know how hard I'd have to swing this thing to go all the way through a door? You just need to focus on the class, focus on helping these students learn]new ways of thinking and talking... very important stuff. The most important thing in your life, without a doubt."

"I want to go home."

"You have three more classes, and I can't get a sub on this short notice! The students must be educated, even on Halloween."

"If Mr. Paba needs to take the day off, he should take the day off," says Daniel Carrol, junior, closeted homosexual.

"Yeah," choruses the class.

"Oh no, one of you locked him in the closet. I will not allow you, whoever you are, to defeat this man. This classroom follows the rule of law, not the rule of anarchy. You will be educated, whether you like it or not!"

I look at Mr. Paba. "Come on," I whisper, "you need to stay. This is your chance to show that you're strong, this is your chance to earn back some of the tremendous amount of respect you've lost." He winces. "For the love of God, man. You're dressed like Superman. Don't be weak. Be a hero."

Mr. Paba stares at me, his sausage-casing costume coated in splinters and sweat and snot. "I want to go home. You can't stop me, even if you are the Principal."

This is the last straw. "If you don't teach, Ray, how can you call yourself a teacher?"

"Are you firing me?" He looks almost hopeful.

"No, no, no, of course not." I couldn't fire someone after they cried in front of a class full of students.

I throw my axe over one shoulder in an attempt to look casual. "If you leave this class, I no longer consider you a teacher. You no longer have that protection."

Mr. Paba looks at the broken pile of door, wiping his nose with his cape. "No offense, Mr. Kent, but I think I'm better off without your protection."

"Please," I say as he walks past me, head down, "call me Adam. We're friends, after all." I can feel a surge of triumph pass from student to student. Eyes brighten up, postures straighten. Students begin talking and laughing with each other as if nothing has happened. As if they're finally enjoying the class. I can't stand it.

I saunter over to Ray's desk, tuck my cape under my butt and sit down. Then I rest my axe on the desk. "ENOUGH!" I yell, in my best and most practiced voice of authority. I spent years in the school bathrooms after hours, yelling myself hoarse at the mirror until I could wield my words like a weapon.

The class quiets immediately. Scooter walks in and begins sweeping up.

"If you don't want to learn, we won't learn. But we won't socialize either. We will stare at the wall until class is over! Learn to like it!"

Chris Hasty, my VP, sighs audibly and leaves.

6.

"Problem solving skills are key to becoming a successful Principal. Over the course of a single day a Principal will encounter numerous obstacles, predicaments and quandaries that grow worse if not handled quickly and correctly. If difficulties and complications ever stack up and threaten to overwhelm you, remember: the simplest solution is the best solution."

I can't help feeling that some students and faculty are looking at me a little differently than usual. I can't quite put my finger on why, but they seem a little wearier, a little less affectionate and open. I hope it's not because I hacked apart Mr. Paba's door the other day. I thought everyone would understand how important it was that he got out of that closet as soon as possible. I guess most people weren't at this school long enough to remember that I keep an axe stashed in my office at all times or the last time I had to use it. I keep it sharp.

Walking around the school and trying to act calm and be present in the moment is difficult when all that's on your mind is where the next Gazette will show up. Tacked to a wall outside the cafeteria? Stacked next to the urinals in the third floor boy's bathroom? Carried by the wind through the quad? It's never the same place twice- Jesse and Tyler are too careful to develop any kind of modus operandi. Any white discarded paper I see palpitates my heart. The constant stress is wearing on my mental and physical health.

What's that grating noise? I look up at the roof of the theater. A small green bird with a hooked beak stands on the corner. I haven't seen that kind of bird around here before. It looks at me and makes the most shrill and discordant noise I've ever heard in my life. Then it does it again.

"What are you? Go away!" I pick up a rock but before I can throw it the bird lets out a piercing shrieks and flies off.

I want some coke.

Woah, where did that come from? I haven't done any in a long time. Now that I think about it, I can't remember the last time I did. Now is not the time to give in to weakness. Now is the time to steady myself, find my center, thicken my skin, and focus on keeping the school running.

First things first: there's a school-wide meeting of the faculty right now, and I need to show up and make it look like I care about their petty grievances and squabbles. I've found that it doesn't really matter what one does during a meeting like that, as long as one keeps their eyes open the whole time and their mouth shut.

I step into the conference room. The heads of the various departments are there already, along with other assorted teachers and staff. Only Sandra Carpenter, the head of the language department, is looking at me in a way I would consider different or stranger than normal. She seems to be scrutinizing me, but looks more perplexed than suspicious or fearful. That's good. I can't afford to let my vicegrip on everyone's goodwill begin to loosen. I must distract them with their own problems, so I can focus on my own.

"Alright, now that Adam is here we can get started," says Chris Hasty, my VP. "Who'd like to go first?"

Everyone raises their hand but Sandra begins speaking immediately. "The language department break room needs to be remodeled. The carpet is old and coming apart, the fridge is twenty years old, and the TV still has a VCR, for God's sake! We deal with these little terrors every day, and I don't think it's too much to ask that we have a decent television and a coffeemaker that wasn't around for the rise and fall of disco."

Ah. Sounds like somebody has a bit of an axe to grind. I can't say I like Sandra, but I admire her honesty. And, if I make her look and feel inferior, it will dissuade others from making such a sniveling public display.

"You know, sometimes I feel that the language teachers don't get enough respect in this facility," Sandra adds. "Or at least our property. Like doors, for instance. Some people seem to have a grudge against those."

A joke? Did she just make a joke about me... to my face? In front of my constituents?

I want to say, "They are my doors, you insufferable pleb! This is my school and everything in it belongs to me! Not you! Choke on your own vomit and die in your sleep, cad!" But, of course, I don't. Despite how immensely satisfying it would be.

Someone snickers. It's one of the tenure dinosaurs so I let it slide. They're probably too deaf to hear what Sandra said anyway, and are just chuckling at her increasingly ridiculous facial expressions.

30

"You're making some valid points, Sandra. The amenities in your department's break room are either seriously lacking or obviously dated. And I will admit, perhaps my decision to rescue Mr. Paba via vigorous application of my axe may have been a bit rushed. I may have been too passionate. Maybe I shouldn't have cared at all that this school's students *locked their teacher in a closet*." I don't shout that last sentence, but I put enough of a growl in my voice that the words hang in the room, echoing in everyone's skulls. I drag out the silence a little longer, letting Sandra fidget as the room unconsciously turns against her, against the miscreant who would dare make light of such a serious issue and question my infallible judgement.

"However, Sandra, the economy has been in a bit of a backslide recently. As you know, English is technically a language as well, and I divvy up what resources I can spare between your two departments." I see Natalie Sanderson, head of the English department, sit up much straighter in her chair. "Normally I would give you both enough money to satisfy your various needs, but I'm afraid the world financial markets are preventing me from doing so. So you see, this semester I can give you a new break room, Sandra... or I can continue to give the English department money for class field trips. I'll let you two work it out amongst yourselves. We're all adults here."

Sandra, effectively shut up for the rest of the meeting, slowly looks over at Natalie. If eyes could shoot fire, she would be burned to a greasy crisp in seconds. Instead, she simply has to weather Natalie's murderous stare until after the meeting when they can make a deal on who will be performing oral sexual favors on who for the rest of the semester. That's how it usually works, I'm sure.

Bernard Maxwell, head of the History department, clears his throat. "We desperately need new textbooks, Mr. Kent."

"Oh yes? Have we had to revise American history recently, Bernard?"

Chuckles spread throughout the room. Bernard smiles weakly. "No, no, of course not. But you see, our current textbooks are viciously sexist. They use the term 'cave men,' you see. These new textbooks use the much more politically correct term 'cave people.' Also, the new edition has many more color pictures. They really help keep the kids interested."

I have enough experience with the textbook industry to know that color ink is tantamount to extortion. Every year the people in charge come out with a new edition of a textbook with all the same text but with pages and pages of new color photographs, and then raise the price. You'd think that buying the last five editions would earn your school some credit with those people. I try to keep my teachers happy, but I can't just buy every new textbook the Texas Board of Education pops out of their collective polluted womb.

"I'll tell you what: we'll let the cave men remain men for now. However, I'll have a substitute teacher come by later in the week and edit out each instance of the phrase with a black marker. How does that sound?"

Bernard stares for second, not expecting his request to be turned down. Obviously, I have failed to keep all of my teachers humble and appreciative of the fact that they have jobs at all. Perhaps if I have some of my students' parents come in and tell teachers like Bernard about the EBT they receive every month their ego won't expect me to give in to their every whim and request. "But the color pictures-"

"Okay, how about this?" I interrupt before he can puke out some sob story about how hard this job is for him, "If anything of dramatic historical relevance happens and we need a new book that includes it, I'll order them. Until then, tell the students to print color pictures off the internet and tape them to the insides of their textbooks. That's called interactive learning, Bernard. Look it up."

Bernard is still struggling to keep me in conversation. "What, what makes an event dramatically historically relevant?"

"If I hear about it on cable news for more than a week. Okay?"

Bernard sighs and nods. He knows the attention span of the news networks. Unless a celebrity is found dead of autoerotic asphyxiation no story gets more than a few

31

day's coverage.

Vicky Cross raises a hand. "The biology department needs more equipment. There are better, state of the art goggles out there that the students need to adequately protect their eyes from dangerous chemicals. And we need more mice to feed to the snakes."

I try not to laugh. I made sure biology or chemistry students haven't even seen a dangerous chemical in years. Whatever educational experience they're missing out on is more than made up for given the fact of how much safer they are. Keeping my students safe is the most important part of my job. Sometimes, it feels like my only job.

"You know, I heard James say the other day that biology is just applied chemistry."

"What?" says James Hetfield, head of the chemistry department. "I mean, technically it is, but-"

" 'Technically'? Biology is more important to the sciences that chemistry is, and you know it!"

"Ah, shut up you two, it's all just applied math!" declares Kendra Brown, head of the math department.

As the argument heats up between the teachers, their funding requests forgotten, I remember that I need to appease the tenure dinosaurs. Nothing much, just a little acknowledgement of their existence and the power that comes from sitting in the same chair for thirty years.

"So yeah, how's the whole tenure thing working out?" They nod, and say nothing.

Well, that's that. I look over at Christ Hasty, my VP, and give him the Look. It involves the eyebrows and the corners of the mouth, and communicates to Chris that he needs to leave the room and then call my cell phone so I have an excuse to leave the meeting early. He and I perform this routine roughly once a week, and we've gotten quite good at it.

Chris nods and stands up, grimly committed to the fact that he'll have to walk back in and deal with the rest of this by himself. He's a very capable man, and the fact that he's indebted to me for his exalted position in the administration doesn't hurt. I couldn't have a better VP. He leaves the room, and a minute later my phone rings.

"Oh, I'm so sorry," I say, glancing at the number. "Urgent business to attend to. Budgets and whatnot. Oh, and the Superintendent too. Please, don't stop talking, I'll be back very shortly."

I shut the door on the arguing teachers and let out a sigh of relief. It lasts exactly two seconds, and then I remember that there are still two students out there who are attempting to burn to the ground everything positive I have brought to this school. Somewhere at this school a sits a stack of Gazettes, hot off the presses, and I can't react in time to prevent at least one or two students from grabbing a copy, reading it, and internalizing their toxic lies. Each paper is contagious and infects the whole of Bayview with its necrotic tissue. And despite this, I will still give them one more chance to repent. Because I love my students. I really do.

I know exactly what class Tyler and Jesse are headed to. I begin my journey through the halls just as the bell rings and the period ends. Rivulets of students pass me as I walk upstream from one end of the school to the other. This is what I need to get my mind off the threats to school security and infrastructure and my own nagging cravings, no doubt induced by the staggering amounts of added stress I'm under. A slice of student life, examined in passing, and changed as I see fit. I just need to mainline a heavy dose of reality. I need to see the evidence of all the hard work and care I put into shaping the students' everyday experience. I need to be reminded of who I am and what I do.

I pass Tyrone Bailey, who I affectionately refer to as the "ticking time bomb" in my mind. I've never seen anyone before who harbors such rage and anger on a daily basis. He moved here his junior year from the Midwest, apparently leaving behind both his circle of friends and an abusive father. He feels anger towards his fellow students, sure, but also for some reason directs a lot of the negative energy at himself. I heard a complaint from one student that he would pull out a lighter in class, keep it lit until the metal was very hot, and then press it into his arm so the whole room smelled faintly of roast pork. He would get into fights with students all the time; but not the geeky, nerdy, dorky or ugly kids like one would expect. Rather, he'd wait until he saw one student bullying another, and he'd beat the bully to near or total unconsciousness. Normally I have a zero tolerance policy when it comes to savage beatings occurring on school property, but I had such admiration for someone who would only pick fights with the biggest and baddest my school had to offer. It impressed me. It also cut the incidents of bullying in the school by half. So, I made sure that he didn't incur any serious judicial sanctions, enrolled him in auto repair and metal shop to keep his hands busy, and told him to talk to a counselor every week. He hasn't gotten in any fights this year, but his presence is enough to put the fear of God in all but the most hardened schoolyard bullies. I do sometimes think I hear a faint ticking emanating from the inside of his cranium, though, counting down to when he needs to vent his emotions again.

I shake his hand. "Hello Tyrone. Still seeing Counselor Cindy on Tuesdays?"

He smiles at me with just his mouth. His eyes jump from me to the students filing past me, seeking to swiftly end any injustice he sees. "Yes sir."

"And you're still being completely candid with her? About the dreams, about your father and mother?"

He nods stiffly, uncomfortable about how well I know him and his personal issues. It's important to remind him about why he's angry all the time, that it's not his fault. It's when he forgets that he starts turning the loathing inward on himself, stoking the furnace inside him even hotter.

"Well alright then. Keep an eye on Daniel in Mr. Volker's metal shop class, okay? I don't want him making any more edged weapons."

I pat Tyrone on the back and continue on, past classrooms and computer labs, past D wing and the drinking fountains. I see Monica Bastida giving dance lessons to a fellow student, walking them through step after step. Listen to the beginnings and ends of various conversations, and grab a couple loose notes off the floor to add to my collection. Stan Birch and Michelle Fowler are kissing each other deeply in front of the band room. I place my hands between them and slowly separate them. "Keep your tongues in your own mouths in the hallways, please. And don't hug too firmly either, it makes some students uncomfortable."

Seconds later, a boy walks past me who catches my eye. It can't be. A homeschooled kid? I can usually pick out a homeschooled kid from a mile away: there's something about how they look at the world that gives them away as different from normal kids. What's he doing here, outside his home school? I put a hand on his shoulder. "Can I help you, son?"

He blinks. "Uh, I'm looking for room C201? I'm supposed to take a test there so I can get into college, the SATs?"

Huh. Well good luck surviving college without the 12 years of social interaction experience public school gives you, I want to say. "Down that hall, third door on the left," I mutter, pat him on the back, and start walking again, past the military recruiters in the quad blasting rap music and holding giant novelty scholarship checks, down the stairs outside the basketball gym, and past the southernmost row of lockers, when I notice Brandon Nelson putting something in his locker. He looks up and widens his eyes when he sees me.

I don't rush but walk right up to him as he shuts his locker. As I finally close the distance between us he puts his hand down the front of his pants and scratches what can only be his scrotum. At my look of disgust he smiles, takes his hand back out, and says, "Hey Mr. Kent. Wanna smell my hand, make sure I haven't been smoking?" he laughs.

I can't deal with this right now. One thing at a time. Disrespecting the Principal to his face is serious matter, but I'm used to that sort of thing from Brandon, and it's more important right now that I stop Tyler and Jesse's assault on everything I hold dear once and for all.

I'm running now, waving at students who greet me as I rush past, eyes firmly on the prize. Up ahead I see Jesse, all alone, putting a book into his backpack. Together, Jesse and Tyler are formidable opponents. They can use the fact that they have the same beliefs, the same unfounded aggression against what I stand for, as evidence that what they are doing is right. Alone, Tyler is weak, unable to look to his friend for guidance and support. He's already unsure of whether what he's doing is worth it, whether it's worth the vengeance I threaten him with mentally every time I look him in the eyes. I just need to put pressure on the fracture, and it will shatter like glass.

"Hello Tyler. Lost any elections recently?"

He nearly drops his book, and swallows. "Yeah, you know that. That's why we have elections, I guess. The people get to choose, not me."

"That's a nice sentiment. What's funny is, you probably would have won, if I hadn't stuffed the ballot box with votes against you!"

One look at my face and he knows I'm telling the truth. His eyes well up a little, but he also looks angry. "How could you do that! That's so wrong! I'll tell-"

"Tell who, Tyler? Who would possibly believe you? Who would ever accept the word of a muckraker like you over the word of a highly accredited Principal? No one, that's who!"

Tyler's breathing heavily now, finding it hard to believe he'd ever face a penalty for his crimes. "Well, I'm not going to stop!"

"Well, then I will continue to make your life more and more miserable until you stop. I can make your life a living hell. Believe me, I've dealt with worse threats to my reign over this school than you."

"That's not right! I thought you cared about your students!"

"You can't win. This isn't a competition or some sort of game. This is real life. This is Bayview High, and as long as I am here, I make the rules, understand? I can't continue to fight with you for the hearts and minds of my students. And you can't continue to do what you're doing and expect there to be no consequences. Serious consequences. It's not worth it, Tyler. It's just not worth it."

"It's a fake newspaper Mr. Kent! It's just a damn joke!"

"Not anymore. Now it's life and death, understand? You still have a chance, you have one choice to make, right now, once and for all. Choose life. Please. Don't do this to yourself."

Tyler's watery eyes widen as true fear begins to set in. "What... what can I do?"

I've finally gotten through to him. He finally understands the error of his ways.

Suddenly Jesse appears, as if from nowhere. "Don't listen to him, Tyler!" he shouts. He looks extremely angry, for some reason. "I heard everything you said! What the fuck is your problem, taking something away Tyler really wants just because of some stupid newspaper? What the hell is wrong with you?"

A fleck of spittle hits my cheek. Jesse dares talk to me like this? Who does he think he is? "I won't allow you to continue talking to me in this way, Jesse. Tyler, explain to him how this works. Tell him-"

"Don't talk to him, Kent. And I heard all the empty threats you made. You can't do shit, do you realize that? We can write whatever we want, and no matter what you do to us, we'll keep writing it. You'll be reading an issue every week till we graduate! How do you feel about that?"

So now it all comes out. They won't stop. They were never going to stop. They'll continue with the Gazette relentlessly unless something is done. "How do I feel about it? How do you feel about the surf club getting shut down, Jesse? How do you feel now that you're responsible for all your friends being unable to surf five days a week?"

Jesse looks like I just punched him in the stomach, but recovers quickly. "You cocksucker. You fucking cocksucker. I bet you like touching little boys, don't you? You pervert, getting all involved in kids' lives. You want to get personal? You have no fucking clue how personal we can get. When we're done, no one in this school will respect you. Because you don't deserve respect. You deserve for everyone to see you for the psychopath you are."

At least they were civil before. Now they're not even pretending to respect me or my position, and somehow, that makes it so much worse. I take a step back from Tyler's rage spit bath, and hold my hands out in a sign of submission. "What did I do, Tyler, Jesse? What did I ever do to deserve all this? Why did you even start?"

Jesse snorts. Tyler speaks up from behind Jesse: "You run this place like a psyche ward, Mr. Kent."

Psych ward. It's actually called the Behavioral Health Unit. You get committed in the emergency room, but Unit is actually another building. You get wheeled there in a chair, even if you can walk. Then you get classified as a "51-50", which means you're committed to the ward for three days, minimum. Every 24 hours after that they review your file and decide whether or not to release you. Every day there's chance you could leave, and every day there's a chance you never will. You see doctors at least once a day. You pace a lot, because really there's nothing else to do and it honestly feels pretty good. You eat your food on trays. You go out for activity time and maybe bounce a basketball, jump rope, do pushups or walk laps around the yard. Sometimes you get called into a side room and do arts and crafts. That's the first and only time you see a girl in the ward. You can read a magazine. Have snack time with decaf coffee and crackers. Pace some more. Every now and then you remember the orderlies putting all your personal belongings into plastic bags.

Your roommate doesn't talk. You try twice but each time he just shakes his head no before you can get out two words, and there's something about the way he looks at you, it makes you realize how invasive it is to talk to somebody when they don't want to talk. He looks haunted or dead. And there's an old guy there who often chooses to wear his underwear as pants.

You're not sure where the exit is, but one door says "AWOL Risk" on it. You try not to stare at it. You are given socks and a hospital gown, but most people keep on the clothes they had on when they got committed, even if it's been three or four of five days. They have free washing machines and soap, so you and the others wash the same set of clothes every day, and you don't need to wear the gown. Then you can still pretend you're not a patient. The socks are nice though. You ultimately keep the socks.

Then pace some more. Go outside. Look at the fence surrounding the yard. Look at the parking lot and some random office building across the street through your room's window. Check in with your doctor. Take the pill.

What is it?

Atavan. It helps. Take it.

What if I don't want to?

You need to. It will make you better.

So you look at the pill and you wonder if it will really help. Help what exactly? Talking to the doctor it suddenly becomes very hard to remember why you're there in the first place.

"This isn't a psyche ward," I say. "You may not like it, but it's nothing like a psyche ward. A psyche ward is a place you couldn't run away from, even if you wanted to. Just leave, you two. Leave the school. Drop out. Get a job. Do whatever you want. But leave now, right now, and don't you dare come back. This is the best I can offer you. This is it."

"What you're saying now just shows how far you've fallen, Kent," snarls Jesse. "You'd rather kick us out than deal with the real problem. I can see how much you really care about your students' safety. Fuck you."

The bell rings. The next period has started. I take one last long look at the two. "Go to class, boys. I'll excuse your tardiness."

I can feel them staring after me as I turn my back on them and walk away. I feel drained- due to my own failure, really. I truly thought I could help these two children, but it's beyond even my power to save them. I wish I knew why they turned out so wrong.

Personally, I feel a school is like the beautiful fruiting body of vast underground organism. All anyone sees of it is just surface. There's so much more intricate work being done, so much growth occurring just under the surface of things, where only the truly knowledgeable can see. Only a select few, the Principals, can change the underpinnings of a thing, while everyone else lives in the thing itself. In nature, some mushrooms pop up miles apart, but they're actually connected underground by a network of fibers: both are actually one inclusive system. However, one or two parasites in the hyphae can kill the whole interconnected ecosystem, and all the beautiful fruiting bodies all over the country. If you find some, you need to weigh the options available to you. What can you do to keep the entire sacred entity alive and flourishing?

When I get to my office, I find a piece of paper with a familiar typeface jammed under the door. The headline reads, "Teacher Raymond Paba's Class Outlawed by Geneva Convention: Too Boring to Sustain Life."

Suddenly, I know what I have to do.

When you murder someone, you need to do it right.

If you use a gun, for example, all you're really doing is moving the trigger. You pull the lever, and someone dies. There's an unhealthy disconnect there, a disparity between the action and consequence. Because it's not your consequence. It's the poor sap getting murdered who pays the consequence.

There was a science experiment once, that asked people what they would do if a runaway train was heading towards a group of five workers on the tracks. Most people asked would pull a lever and change the train's path so it only ran over one worker on the other track, rather than the five the train would have killed. But, when asked if they would push someone off the bridge above the tracks in order to stop the train with their body, very, very few said that they would. It's the same amount of lives saved and lost in both situations, the only difference is that in one example you end someone's life by pulling a lever, in the other you actually have to push them off a bridge. For some reason it seems like one is murder, and the other isn't.

It's for this reason I feel that using a gun to kill someone is too easy. I'm not saying you should choke the guy to death, and I'm not saying you should look them in the eyes as the life leaves them. That's morbid. But you should definitely get hands-on with it. Gain an appreciation for the act of death. It doesn't get easier. It does, however, get more meaningful.

School's out for the day. It's been over an hour since the last bell, and I'm prepared for what I have to do. I put on my calfskin gloves, adjust my collar and tie, shoot my cuffs, and walk to Mr. Paba's class, rope coiled tightly in my hands. He usually stays in his classroom for four to five hours after school's over, simply because he has nothing to go home to but a television, a microwave dinner, and the utter lack of satisfaction at a job well done.

I knock on the door and then let myself in. Mr. Paba is sitting at his desk, alone. The class is empty, and I notice for the first time how bare the walls are, as well as the stack of ungraded tests piled on the floor. Coffee stains fleck his shirt, his hair is uncombed, and his teeth are brown and stink. This is a man who no longer cares about his job, his hygiene, or his life.

"Hello Mr. Kent," Mr. Paba sighs, bored out of his skull. He glances at the rope in my hand, and then back at the computer screen.

"Please Raymond, we're friends. Call me Adam."

"Okay... Adam. How are you?"

"Not good, Ray. Can I be completely candid with you?"

Raymond nods, interested now. Graphs of the historical price of gold flicker on his computer screen, forgotten.

"The school is crumbling around me. Everything I've built here is crashing down around my feet. Two of your students, Jesse and Tyler, are responsible. Have you read the most recent issue of what they call... the Gazette?"

I toss the paper on his desk. He reads the headlines, and winces slightly. "Well, they obviously don't like my teaching style very much."

"They don't like anything, Raymond. They hate all life. They live only to see me in excruciating mental anguish. Spreading lies about my policies, condemning me, and slandering my school! If something isn't done soon, all of my students will begin to think just like them. I will be unable to teach, unable to keep them safe. The entire system will fail!"

Mr. Paba clutches the desk. He obviously didn't care much about the paper, but he can tell how worried I am, how close I am to the edge. "Can't you just make them stop?"

"I can't. They're my students. I can't really hurt them. I have to be the bigger man. I have to be the adult. And they... they won't stop until I'm dead. I'm sure of it."

"Sounds like there's nothing you can do."

"Exactly. That's why you're going to do something for me, Ray. You're going to save the school."

"I am?" Mr. Paba scratches his scalp, looking thoughtful. "What do you want me to do?"

"You need to kill yourself."

He stares at me. His mouth hangs open. "What?"

"It's the perfect solution. You kill yourself next to this copy of the Gazette." I hold it up and shake it. "Tyler and Jesse think that their writing provoked you into ending your life, and they stop writing altogether, just so no one else gets hurt. The guilt will be too much. They won't be able to write another word!"

"I can't do that!" Sweat beads on his forehead. He looks around, unsure if I am serious.

"You have nothing to live for. Look at me, Ray. Look at me." I stare directly into his eyes and put my face an inch from his. "You are no longer a teacher, remember? You failed your students on Halloween. You have absolutely nothing in your life worth living for."

"That's... that's not true..." he gasps. Mr. Paba's voice is getting weaker, fainter.

"This school is under attack. The whole system will fail if something is not done. Today. Now is the time to give it all, to be a part of something greater than yourself. Now is the time to truly be a part of Bayview High. Be strong, Ray. Be a hero. For once in you fat, miserable life, take a stand for what you believe in."

Mr. Paba is really sweating now, still clutching the desk with white knuckled hands. He stares at me still, barely moving.

"Everyone will think about you, everyone will say your name. Hundreds, thousands of people will feel sad that you're gone. Some will cry even. You'll *matter*. You'll actually matter to your fellow human beings. You'll have a profound effect on everyone, no matter what they thought of you when you were alive."

"I-"

"Be honest, Ray. Be honest with me. Do you really think you can handle life the way it is, all alone, loved by no one, for just one more day? Have some dignity. You're not a teacher anymore, Ray. You're nothing, and you'll always be nothing unless you do this."

Mr. Paba looks around, studying the bare walls of the classroom. "Words hurt me so much."

"No one will make fun of you anymore."

He lets go of the desk, and suddenly appears very relaxed. "Okay, Mr. Kent. I'll do it. For you. For the school."

"Call me Adam, Ray. Please. Now put this on," I say, holding up an adult diaper.

Mr. Paba pushes it away. "A diaper? Are you making fun of me? Don't make fun of me! Don't you even think about making fun of me now!"

"Ray, Ray, Ray. I'm not making fun of you. Do you know what people do after they die? They void their bowels. Everyone does, no matter their lot in life. Do you know how hard it is to get the smell of human feces out of a room, especially if it's been soaking into the carpet all night?"

"N-No...."

"A long time, Ray. The classroom will be unusable for weeks. Children will miss out on their education, far too much. And the paramedics who take away your body? Scooter the janitor, who'll clean up after? They'll thank you, Ray. Vehemently. They'll think you're the most thoughtful person ever, willing to wear a diaper so he doesn't make a mess of things. Keeping others in mind, even after your spirit has left."

Mr. Paba still looks unsure. I hold out the diaper, and say in a special Voice I've practiced for years: "Put it on."

He complies, sliding his legs one at a time into the leg holes. I had to get the largest size diaper I could find. An overweight man in an oxford shirt, khakis, and an adult diaper looks absolutely ridiculous, more than I thought was already possible. But I don't laugh. This is the most serious thing I have ever done.

"Alright, now stand on the chair," I say as I climb onto his desk. Mr. Paba does so, then stares at the ceiling with glassy eyes.

"Have I told you that I believe in heaven, Ray?" I say, as I grab one end of the rope.

"Really?"

"Yes I do. And I know for a fact that the good that comes of your actions here today? The countless lives it will save? That will get you into any heaven, in any religion."

"Well, not really. I used to be a Mormon, and any Mormons who leave the church go to hell. Even people who never believed in the first place have a chance to get into heaven, but not us. That's what they told us all the time, anyway. I'm going to hell after this." He says this with no discernible emotion in his voice.

I pause, considering this rule. "Well, I used to be a Catholic. And let me tell you something. I myself was told many times that people who commit suicide go to hell," as I say this I push up one of the foam ceiling tiles and start tying the end of the rope around the metal beam in between. "But I don't believe that. No matter how many times I was told. That's one of the reasons I left the church. I feel that if a person commits suicide for the right reasons, for the greater good, for children... they get into heaven after they die. No matter what."

Mr. Paba stops looking at the ceiling and instead looks up to me as I stand on his desk. "Do you really believe that, Mr. Kent?"

"Of course I do. You're my friend. I would never lie to a friend." The final knot almost tied.

"Do I get a plaque? With my name, and all my accomplishments?"

"More than that. I'll put your name on the scoreboard. Everyone will see your name at every game. I'll reposition the stadium lights to illuminate it more than anything else in the stands. You will become synonymous with football victory. Our team's going to win it all this year, you know. We *will* defeat Lincoln High!"

"And my picture. I want my face on it, three feet high."

I grit my teeth. "Deal. Anything you want, Ray. This is all for you. Now hold still." I already tied the hangman's knot in my office so all I do now is place the loop around his neck, then cinch it firmly. I hop off the desk and stand on the ground, looking up at him.

"Are you ready?"

Mr. Paba stands there on the chair, and then looks down at his diaper. "Adam?"

"Yeah?"

"I don't want to do this yet. I need some time to think about this."

"Ray, don't say that. You're about to do this school a service I can never truly repay. Everyone here will owe you their livelihoods, and their lives."

"But how do I know you'll even put my name on the scoreboard?" He bends his knees and places his hands on the desk.

"Well, you might be in a position to negotiate if I hadn't already put the noose around your neck," I say, and kick the chair.

The man falls backward, away from the desk. His eyes bug out as the rope snaps taut. The sounds he makes reminds me of someone trying to chew and swallow something they took too big a bite of. His feet flail back and forth, a foot and a half off the ground. A shoe flies off. Now he's trying to get his chubby fingers at the noose, but it's cutting so deeply into his neck fat that one can barely see the rope sunk into the canyon of his triple chins.

"Ack! Huuuck! Awwwk!"

"Shhh... relax. Think about the school. You be able to watch how well we're all doing, up in the clouds, next to God. Stop struggling. It's all over. It's done. Embrace it."

Now Mr. Paba kicks at the desk, trying to get his feet some leverage on top. The toe of his one remaining shoe taps the edge of the desk but can't grip. He kicks at the desk again and again. His face is a shade between beet red and eggplant purple. He's got some fingers somehow wedged slightly under the noose. "Helllkkk... helllk!"

"Okay, that's enough," I say. I grab both feet and pull him away from the desk. The rope is now at about a forty-five degree angle with the ceiling, and the metal bar it's attached to begins to bend slightly.

Mr. Paba's cheeks puff out, and his neck seems to swell. He digs his fingers even further under the rope, pulling so hard I can actually see the tendons in the back of his hands.

"Stop it! Just stop it!" I'm yelling now. I lean back, grip his ankles, and pull even harder.

Snap! The metal bar supporting the rope breaks free of the ceiling, bent nearly in half. Mr. Paba drops like a three hundred and fifty pound stone. The side of his head just kisses the edge of his desk. There's a truly massive thump as he lands.

He starts coughing and coughing, his eyes rolling wildly around and up into his head. His head is gushing from hitting the desk, and as he coughs he shakes his whole body, spattering the walls and soaking the carpet with blood.

"NO NO NO!" I scream. "NO!" I place one hand on the back of Mr. Paba's head, and one on his chin. Then I twist his neck until it snaps. He finally goes limp. He finally stops making those noises. I drop him to the floor.

I can't breathe. My vision is red at the edges, and I'm seeing stars too. This doesn't look like he hung himself! I twist his neck back around so he's facing the front again. I get some blood on my gloves, and on the cuffs of my suit. No good. It's all wrong looking. "Look what you made me do!" I scream.

I punch him in the face once, then twice. His nose, now pointed flat off to one side, starts bleeding. I start breathing again. Mr. Paba stares at me, red veined eyes sunk deeply into his swollen face, which is actually getting paler by the second.

"Sorry. I shouldn't have punched you. That was unnecessary."

I get unsteadily to my feet. My head is pounding. The pain is so intense I can't think. I look around the room. There's a hole in the ceiling, blood flecks on the walls and a pool of blood in the carpet. Mr. Paba lies wearing one shoe and a diaper, one end of a rope around his neck, the other tied to a bend metal frame on the ground. His nose runs dripping crimson liquid. I can't find the other shoe.

What do I do now? What can I do? Bleach out the stains, maybe somehow fix the hole in the ceiling? Mr. Paba has no friends or family, everyone would probably just think he ran away. What's important is getting the bloodstains out. Is it even possible to get that much blood out of carpet? Maybe I could just cut out the carpet, and roll Mr. Paba up in it. Would it soak into the floor underneath?

I look back at the man. It's broad daylight, and I'd have to drag that huge bloody lump pretty far to get to my car. And there's no way I could hide that man in my trunk.

"I just killed a man," I say to the empty room. I suddenly feel very tired. Well, no sense dwelling on the past. I'm going to bed. I'll deal with all this in the morning.

7.
"A successful Principal works well with others."

I wake up to the phone ringing. Outside my window the sun isn't quite up yet. "Hello?"

"Mr. Kent, this is Scooter. I'm a janitor at your school."

"Of course I remember you, Scooter. I know every one of my janitorial staff. Did you enjoy Yom Kippur?"

"Yes, sir. That's not why I called though."

"I understand. It's very early. This must be important."

"I found Ray Paba in his room this morning. Looks like he hung himself, then the ceiling broke from all the weight. I'm not sure you'll believe me, but he looks to be wearing an extra large adult diaper. It could be those magic Mormon underpants they're supposed to wear."

I wait to see if he'll volunteer any more information, then say, "Oh no. Not Raymond! I'm terribly distraught right now!" I pause, unsure of what to say next. "I was at home all night, you know. If only I could have been there, if only I could have intervened!"

"So, uh... should I call the police?"

"How does he look?"

"Sir?"

"How does he look? Is it messy? Does he look peaceful?"

"His neck looks funny. And there's blood everywhere, not quite sure how that came about."

I drum my fingers on my knee. "Call the police. I'll be right there."

When I arrive the police are already there. I make sure my tie is tight as I walk purposefully up to the police tape. A woman in uniform is outside the classroom door.

She holds up her hand. "No one but police."

I stand my ground. "I am the Principal of this school. Everyone here reports to me. Your job will be much easier if I know what's going on."

She sighs. Then she picks up a pair of white plastic shoe wraps. "Put these on. Crime scene techs are going to check for shoe prints."

Shoe prints? I hadn't thought of that. Can they match shoe prints like finger prints? I had new carpeting installed two years ago, hopefully the students' shoes have worn it down enough so that it no longer holds an impression. I put on the booties and open the door.

Inside, the scene is exactly as I left it, except for the two other living people inside. Raymond is on the floor next to the desk. His neck is purple and his face more bloated that usual. Dried blood pools around his head and is sprinkled on the desk and dry-erase board. The rope curves around his body and terminates at the bent ceiling bar.

He soiled his diaper since I last saw him. The diaper was a wise move.

40

A short stubby man wearing a crumpled mohair suit and camel trench coat talks to a uniformed officer halfway down the rows of desks and chairs. They both have plastic on over their shoes.

They both look at me, confused. The uniformed officer moves to remove me from the scene, but the other man (a Detective?) puts a hand on her shoulder.

"One minute," he grunts, and then looks at me, scratching his cheek. "Are you the Principal?"

"My name is Principal Kent," I reply, and shake his hand.

"Excellent. Jenny, why don't you go outside and take the janitor's statement."

Jenny shrugs and walks outside. As soon as she leaves, the Detective hunches slightly and leans in close to me. "I'm going to be completely candid with you, as one professional to another. Can I ask you to do the same?"

I nod.

"Well, Principal Kent, my name-"

"Please, call me Adam."

"... Adam, my name is Detective Cooper. Call me Detective. What can you tell me about the deceased?"

I take another look at the body. "Honestly? He's overweight. Depressed. Pathetic. Incapable of doing his job and unable to change. Unmarried. Childless. And completely unoriginal when it comes to Halloween costumes."

"I see," says Cooper, writing on a notepad.

I add, "It's no wonder he killed himself."

"Oh," says Cooper, looking up. "He didn't kill himself."

I force myself to appear relaxed, but my eyes narrow and brow wrinkles anyway. "No? It looks like he did."

"I agree that to the untrained eye this looks like a suicide. But I am not an untrained eye, I am a policeman. This suicide was staged, and very poorly at that."

I take offense to that and hope it doesn't show. "How can you tell, Detective?"

"Come closer and I'll show you. Don't step on the blood spatter."

We walk over to Raymond's body and both crouch down. I cover my nose and mouth.

"Ahh, you get used to that smell after your first year on fucking homicide, I'll tell you that." Cooper laughs, and then coughs a smoker's cough. After half a minute, he recovers and continues, "I can't tell you exactly how he died, that's the medical examiner's job. All that CSI: Miami bullshit aside, though, I can tell you that Ray here didn't do this by himself.

"First," he points to the wound on Raymond's head, "when he hit his head on the desk he was still alive. Body's been dead more than a few hours, it wouldn't spurt blood like that. Second," he points to his neck, "see that bruising, the odd angle? His neck's been broken. Can't break your neck with a rope just standing on a chair, you need a long fall, gallows style. Third," he points to Ray's nose, "His nose is broken, if not when he died, then immediately after."

Cooper takes a breath. Muffled by my hand, I manage to get out a "that's terrible".

And it is. He's convinced that this is a homicide. The damage this will do to the students' sense of safety will be severe.

"Is it possible he hung himself, died, then fell and broke his nose and neck on the desk?"

"Nope. Neck looks twisted, and it's impossible to break your neck from such a short fall."

"But he's so fat!"

"Didn't happen. Here's how I think it went down." He stands up, and brings his fingers together in a square in front of his face like a director framing a scene. "The perp forces Mr. Paba to string himself up at gunpoint. The perp kicks the chair over but the

41

stubborn fuck won't die. Maybe his neck's too chubby. So the perp pulls on his legs to hasten the process. That's why his socks are all bunched up and one shoe's missing. The added force breaks the ceiling, he hits his head on the desk. Then the killer gets all hands-on and sadistic. He abuses him verbally, forces him to put on a diaper. Then, when he's had his fun, he snaps his neck like *so*," Cooper makes a motion like he's turning a large corkscrew, "and then savagely breaks his nose out of spite. This murderous demon must have really hated the poor fat fuck. Yes, this crime was motivated by pure unadulterated hatred. I guarantee it."

He's scrutinizing me now for any sort of emotion, any kind of tell, like a poker player trying to discern a good or bad hand. I try to look shocked by his portrayal of rage and violence. "Hatred? I truly didn't like the man. Nobody here did. But I didn't hate him. Who could have hated him so much?"

"Anyone. Anyone is capable of murder. That's why my job exists."

"Anyone?" I see an opening. "Could it have been the janitor?"

"That old geezer? Now way. He's too frail for this kind of strongarmed brutality. Whoever killed this man was pretty muscular. The intense anger and adrenaline didn't hurt either. Besides, he's not a killer. I can tell if someone's a killer just by looking in their eyes."

I resist the temptation to ask him about this supposed skill.

"Yep. Comes from years and years of experience. Once I meet the murderer face to face? I'll know." He looks around the room, as if suddenly realizing it's empty, and then crouches next to me, his face close. His breath stinks. I can see grease spots on his yellow and black striped silk tie. It makes him look like a dirty wasp.

"Remember what I said about being completely candid? One professional to another?"

I nod, removing my hand from my nose to show how serious I am. The scent of excrement fills my nostrils.

Cooper looks around one more time. "I have no leads. The crime scene techs might find something, a print or a hair, but I doubt it. I don't know anything about the victim. And anything I do learn about him will be secondhand, tainted by others' fear of police. That's what I like about you. You're not afraid of me, and you're honest." I nod again, trying not to retch.

"I need your help. I need to know if he had any enemies. This is a crime of passion. Who would want to hurt him? You know the victim intimately, and you know the suspects better than I ever could. And I know, I *know*, that this was done by somebody at the school. I need your knowledge, Adam."

I pretend to take a moment to think this offer over. "Of course I will help you, Detective. If the killer is still at the school, if what you say is true... I want them to answer for their crime as much as you. Until the killer is found, my students are at risk, and I cannot allow that."

"Good to hear!" His voice changes slightly. There is pleading in it now. "Any help you can give me would be appreciated. Any rumor, any whisper, any mention of Raymond at all. I just... I don't even know where to start! Without motive I won't be able to convince a jury. Forensic evidence will take weeks, maybe months it's so backed up. If I don't have a suspect in custody within forty eight hours, I never will."

I show a shaky smile, the smile of someone still reeling from the death of a friend. "I'll ask around. I'll have to ask you to not follow me, though. Please, conduct your investigation as you see fit, but if people see you with me they might not want to talk. But alone, one on one, they trust me. I'm the Principal."

He looks relieved. "Can I count on you to testify in court, if it comes to that? This is your school after all. Legally your word is golden."

At that moment I realize what I must do, and how I must do it. I can't help the small smile on my face.

"I will tell the truth, the whole truth, and nothing but the truth. So help me God."

When Cooper turns his head to hack up more phlegm I reach over and pull out a clump of Raymond's hair. Then Cooper and I leave the classroom together before splitting up, both complicit in the same crime and both dedicated to seeing some ultimate form of justice carried out.

Now I know what I must do. I realize that I have very little time to accomplish it. I run through the empty pre-class halls. The school day will start in less than an hour and once word gets out about Raymond all Hell will break loose. Students and faculty will be terrified. I will be looked to for comfort and reassurance. The only way this event doesn't hurt the school beyond all repair is if I can produce a culprit. Or two culprits.

I go to my evidence room first, with its shelves of confiscated materials, and reach under a pile of pornographic playing cards for the small baggie of cocaine hidden underneath. Then I run to my office, and from my desk I grab my blood flecked leather gloves.

Everything I've done at this school was mandated by necessity. This is no exception. I need this plan to work, truly and utterly. It's not my job on the line. It's my livelihood. My reason for living. My life.

I rush out of my office and almost run into a group of teachers. One speaks up: "Adam, why are there police here?"

"Sorry, important business!" I yell, turning one hundred and eighty degrees and running at full sprint. I have very little time until my precious students arrive. They are smart. As soon as they get here, they will know something is wrong. Already a few of the early arrivals mill about nervously, sensing something amiss.

I arrive at Jesse's locker, unlock it with my master key and fling the door wide. Inside are textbooks, loose papers, a bag of chips, spare glasses, and some quarters. Pencils, pens, chapstick. And now, a baggie of cocaine.

"You brought this on yourself." I whisper, slamming the door shut. The prospect of what I'm doing makes me hesitate. Then I force myself to remember each time I gave Tyler and Jesse a chance to stop. It warms my belly and clears my head of any nagging doubts.

I hear footsteps and anxious chatter: more students. They cannot see me here. I dash down C-wing in the opposite direction. I lunge into a bathroom and hide inside a stall until my heartbeat and breathing slow. Don't rush things. Make sure the job is done right. Someone has written on the white tile "BLANK WALLS = BLANK MINDS".

Keeping close to the wall, I peer around the corner at the wall of lockers. Tyler's is among them. Gary Gasp and Marian Lee stand in front, idly chatting. I approach them slowly. When I'm up close, I throw my arms around their shoulders.

"Hello Chris, Debbie! I'm going to have to ask you to go to class now."

"But school hasn't started yet!" Chris whines.

"I know. Please understand: it... is... not... safe... out... here." I enunciate each word, tightening my grip on the Golden Couple with each one.

"Why?" asks Debbie.

"Your teacher will tell you. Now get to class. I need to know that you're safe."

If I don't do my job perfectly, everyone will think there's a killer roaming the halls. Even if there isn't, really. I unlock Tyler's locker and toss in my gloves. I wore latex gloves underneath so there are no fingerprints inside. I gently wipe the outside off with a wet paper towel from the bathroom, leaving the blood stains. I then top them off with Raymond's hair.

It wasn't about you and me, Tyler. It was about the school. About what's good for the collective. But then you made it personal. You made it me versus you. If you force my hand and make me take the gloves off, they will come off. No holds barred.

One last task.

I check the clock on the wall. It reads 7:19AM. 11 minutes. I just have to hope Tyler and Jesse don't check their lockers before school.

I enter the nearest classroom. Madeline Allman looks up from the board she's

43

writing sample equations on.

"Your computer, is it connected to the network?" I ask.

"Well hello to you to," she says. "I saw police cars in the parking lot. Is this something I should worry about?"

"No. They will be brought to justice."

She hesitates. "What?"

I grind my teeth. "Is it connected to the network, Madeline?"

"Of course-"

I stop listening to her and sit at her computer. Melissa Pinkerton said I just needed a teacher's password and username and I could change that teacher's grades with impunity. I know Raymond's username: rPaba. But his password... what could it be? Could it be the default password I gave him when he first became a teacher seven years ago and was too lazy to change?

I'm in. But I have only a few minutes. I pull up his grades list and scan the names. 'Tyler Dourden- A'. A few clicks, and the 'A' becomes an 'F'. I look for Jesse, and change his grade from an A to an F as well. I contemplate the "save" button. I'm just doing my job, and I aim to keep it. I'm the Principal. I can only help those who are willing to accept it.

I hit the "save" button. It's done. I can't take the time to ponder what I just did, though. Tyler and Jesse might already have their lockers open.

Where's the Detective? I think. I realize I have no idea where he could be. I leave the classroom. The students I see look uneasy. They want to know what's going on and it kills them that they don't. I go to the main entrance, but the Detective's not there. Then the cafeteria. It's empty. Then the east parking lot. He's there, just staring at the students who walk by.

His face is grim, and when he sees me it gets grimmer. "Lots of potential killers here."

That expressionless statement hits me like a punch to the stomach. I raise my students right. They are caring, decent, and good. Who is he to judge them so harshly?

"I have good news, Detective. Well, good and bad."

"Yeah?" He's as eager as a hungry dog. "Fuckin' A man, just tell me already!"

"It seems that two of Mr. Paba's students may have been involved in his death."

Cooper smiles, baring yellow teeth. "That's what I'm talking about! Give me names. Give me a motive."

"They were doing very badly in his class. Very bad grades."

"That's not enough for motive. You know these two kids, yeah? Did they give any sign that they meant Mr. Paba harm?"

"They wrote a very emotionally distressing newsletter recently. They called him a 'shambling, drooling idiot without a single instructive gene on his corpulent body' and a 'fat sack of pus with no redeeming qualities'. They truly hated him and verbally excoriated him at every opportunity."

"Ehhh... those are just words. They sounds like angry students with poor grades. And I want to believe you, I really do. But if you can't convince me, you'll never convince a jury."

I can feel the bow I've neatly wrapped around this incident coming rapidly undone. Raymond's death needs closure and a clean conclusion now or it will mar my students' psyches forever.

"If you were to search their lockers now, before they do, like literally in the next 120 seconds, you would very likely find material evidence directly linking these two students to the homicide."

Cooper's eyes glitter like a rat's. "That would be very nice. Yes. Very nice. Save me lots of work if I can catch them now..."

"All the evidence you need, Detective. But you need to get your people and take action immediately."

Cooper snaps out of his reverie. He places a hand on my shoulder. "If what you say turn out to be true, you have my undying thanks for bringing these cunt rags to justice. I owe you big time."

"Let me sit in on the interview at the station? They trust me. I can make them confess."

"You got it." He calls over the officers and they hurtle toward the quad. I shout the locker numbers and locations as they disappear from view. I can see one of the police has a bright red bolt cutter.

The school bell rings. Now the longest day of my career can begin.

I spend the next few hours trying to keep the school day from becoming a total loss. First, I call an emergency teacher meeting with the heads of all the departments.

"I have grave news. You have already seen the police and are no doubt wondering what's going on. I regret to inform you that Raymond Paba is dead."

The teachers gasp collectively.

"Heart attack," says James Hetfield, matter-of-factly.

"Actually, no. He was murdered."

"Oh my God!" wails Sandra Carpenter. She begins crying. Others join in.

"Now, now, I know this is troubling information. But I think it's important to keep in mind what Raymond would want. He's a humble man, and wouldn't want us to make a big fuss about this."

"A big fuss! A big fuss! We're all in danger!"

"The police have two suspects in custody. Everything is fine."

They continue crying.

"I hope for the sake of your students that the crying stops as soon as you leave the room."

What's wrong with these people? Don't they understand that his death was the most positive thing to happen to Raymond in his entire life? Don't they know that this collective show of mania just freaks out the students?

"Who did they arrest?" asks Riccardo Sandoval, head of the Spanish department.

"That's confidential. Just rest easy that justice has been served, and get back to the job at hand. The number one thing the students need right now is to be distracted from their thoughts and feelings, preferably for the entirety of the day. That is your noble mission. If you need two minutes to collect and compose yourself, I understand. But make it a quick two minutes. Dismissed."

I understand now that I cannot depend on the teachers to adequately communicate to the students what the current situation is. Nothing is more disruptive and shocking than seeing your teacher unable to control their emotions. Ideally, the teachers would be strong, put up a united front, and most importantly stop crying and being so afraid like little toddlers screaming at the sight of their own shadow.

Christ Hasty, my VP, finishes showing the staff the door, whispering soothing nothings as they leave. "Schedule an emergency assembly, Chris. I need to address my people and assuage their fears."

"I think that's a good idea. How soon?"

"Next period. And while you're at it, check if Raymond had any life insurance. The school parking lot needs to be repaved." Chris nods and walks away.

I am alone. My thoughts wander. Why don't I feel happy? I should. I just solved my two biggest problems in one day. And best of all, none of my students were hurt. Still, something is nagging at me. It feels like I've left some great work of art unfinished and I don't know why.

I exit the conference room. Patrick Cena, sophomore, leans against a display case decorated with multicultural collages of togetherness. His eyes look haunted, and his body language says he could collapse at any moment.

"Patrick? You look awful! What's wrong?"

He stares at me, and then past me. "Someone killed Mr. Paba, Mr. Kent."

"But it's not your fault, is it?" Now he looks terrified. "Of course it isn't! You have nothing to worry about!"

"It's not that..."

"Don't tell me you miss him!" I say, incredulous. "You hated his class. You were sent to my office at least five times because he couldn't handle your taunts, class disruptions, and verbal abuse. You no longer have to sit through another period of soul-death. You should be happy!"

Patrick's eyes well up. "I didn't know this back then, but now that he's gone I realize that I actually looked forward to that class. Having a teacher like Mr. Paba, it brought the class together. It turned into a community. Mr. Kent, you have no idea how fun it is to rally together against something. We'll share the experience for the rest of our lives. We only teased him because we liked him. We hated him, but we liked him too."

He's right. I don't understand that at all. I should have known that rosy nostalgia would twist and blur their true feelings towards him. Now that he's gone, they miss him, and their young minds can't remember all the arduous torture they suffered in his class.

"Chin up, Patrick." I pat him affectionately. "It will take time, but soon you'll have forgotten all about him."

"But I want to remember him."

"No you don't. Now I expect to see you at the assembly next period. Everything will be better once you hear my words."

Patrick shows a half smile.

The entire school is arrayed before me. I can feel tension in the air. Tension and fear. For a second, I envision Tyler and Jesse being led to a patrol car. I shudder with pleasure. Pleasure and... a slight uneasiness. A passing consideration that somehow justice has not truly been done yet. I shake it off. In public speaking, confidence is everything, and I can't let my near brush with disaster show in my face or posture. Far from being visibly weakened, this experience has actually made me stronger than ever. The school needs a hero to look to in times of fear and darkness. It's my job to be the hero. Always has been.

I breathe into the microphone. The chatter ceases.

"It is with deepest sorrow that I must confirm that the rumors are true. Raymond Paba, beloved teacher, died sometime yesterday. He was 37." A few sharp intakes of breath from those who were unaware. Possibly some barely audible snickering from the far back.

"We must be strong in this time of tribulation. Raymond would not want us to be sad on his account. Rather, I know for a fact that Ray would want us to move on with our lives and focus entirely on academics. We would all be unwise to allow flawed emotion to distract us from what we are meant to do every minute we are at this school: learn something new. Focus on building relationships with the living, not needlessly reliving moments with those gone from our reach."

I look steadily from left to right, absorbing their rapt faces. "Raise your hand if you are scared."

Arms appear like masts in a harbor.

"Please hear this clearly so there is no doubt: there is no need to be scared. No logical reason. The police have suspects in custody right now."

Cries of "who?" flutter about.

"I cannot comment further. Understand that no one takes the threat of violence on this campus more seriously than I. New policies will be enacted to ensure the safety of students and faculty. New security guards. Metal detectors. Staff to monitor the campus's security system 24/7. Just to name a few. The truth is that there is nothing to be scared of. It makes no sense to be afraid of something beyond your control.

"I am not just saying these things to give you false hope. You will die someday." I let this sink in. "You may die of natural causes or by accident. That is out of our control. I'm not going to tell you otherwise or lie to you. But do not feel fear. I swear there will never be another murder at this school. The only person who can kill you here is God. No one else has more power than me at Bayview High."

No more snickering or hyperventilating. It may be my imagination, but I feel the assembled crowd relax and breathe easier. The fear lifts away like light lace in the wind.

"We will get through this together, and only together. Provide comfort and consolation to your peers. And then, as a group, forget Ray entirely. It's what he would have wanted. Thank you."

For an instant I think I hear Ray's choked pleas but it is quickly drowned out by the applause.

After the assembly I leave Chris Hasty in charge and drive to the police station. It's a single story building with a gunmetal gray metal roof and a front of mirrored tempered glass. Potted ferns flank double doors that read "8th Precinct" and "Metro PD". I walk up to Reception. The woman behind the desk stares at me. Perhaps my suit and tie have thrown her for a loop.

"Is Detective Cooper around?"

"Yes, but he's busy right now. What is this regarding?"

"Two of my students were arrested this morning. I'm greatly concerned for their welfare."

"I'll let him know. Please take a seat."

I sit in a poorly padded chair. To my left is a man with tattoos on his neck, hands, knuckles, and scalp. To my right sits a woman in a low cut halter top and short cutoffs, ignoring her daughter rocking back and forth next to her. The mother is texting with long fake nails. I feel uncomfortable here. My job may give me respect here, but no jurisdiction. I find myself absentmindedly checking my cuffs for bloodstains.

"Adam!" says a raspy voice.

I look up at Detective Cooper, stand, and extend my hand. "I'm glad to see you, Detective. What's the situation?"

He's wearing the same coat and suit, but they're more stained now. He has a manilla folder under his arm. "Just waiting for you. Always the professional, I remembered your request and have kept the two juveniles sweating in the interview rooms for the last few hours with no outside contact. They'll sing like fucking birds." He licks his lips and rubs his palms. Sweat drips down his temples. He smells like stale charcoal.

"Here's how I'm conducting the interrogation. I speak to them first. You just sit quiet and be the familiar authority figure. If you want to intimidate them with your eyes, go for it. Then after I give the signal you get to ask them questions. Remember, we're trying to get a confession here. They need to say they were at the scene. If they explain why, even better. But legally, we just need them to admit they were in that classroom yesterday."

"I understand. I want the truth as much as you do."

"Oh, we'll get the truth. I don't think you're really necessary here, but just in case I can't break them you'll have to back me up. Finish strong. Let's go in and get this fucking done!"

We walk up to a door marked "Interview A". I can see Tyler inside, his face buried under crossed arms. Cooper licks his lips again and pushes his way in.

"Mr. Dourden," he says, sitting down and tossing the folder on the table. The walls are a sickly green-white and all the lights are blinding fluorescents. A mirror runs the length of one wall. I can feel a camera here as well, recording the whole thing. There's no clock.

Tyler looks at me. "Mr. Kent!" His face is pale, his eyes red. His hands tremble.

"I'll be conducting this interview, Mr. Dourden. Mr. Kent is just here to observe."

He points at Tyler. "Do you know where you are?"

Tyler glances back at me.

"Don't look at him. Look at me."

"I'm in the police station."

"Yes, but more specifically?"

"The interview room?"

Cooper sighs. "You're in Homicide division."

What color is left in Tyler's face washes away.

"I just want to ask you a few questions. Just help clear a few things up. No one's accusing you of anything. Relax."

My student nods.

"Where were you last night?"

"I was at my house, with my parents."

"Can they confirm this?"

"I can call them right now. Actually, I'd really like to call-"

"Soon."

I'm not a lawyer, but I know that Tyler can call a lawyer anytime he wants. I also know minors need to be accompanied by a lawyer or a relative when they've been apprehended. I admire Cooper's disregard for procedure. He desperately wants the truth. Or a promotion. Or a "solved" case to add to his batting average.

"Did you make any calls that would show up on anyone's phone? Make any purchases with the time on the receipt?"

Tyler shakes his head. I feel some relief.

"When did you last talk to Jesse Corvall?"

"I don't remember. Yesterday at school."

Cooper's head bobs up and down. "So you and Jesse were together yesterday, around 3pm?" Does Cooper know the time of death? I wonder if Raymond's been taken to the medical examiner yet.

"Yes."

"And yesterday afternoon, after school? Were you together?"

"Yeah, we went to the beach."

"Can anyone confirm that story?"

"We didn't see anyone we knew there. Wait, Jesse can tell you we were there!" He brightens up at the prospect of Jesse going to bat for him and getting out of here. I usually hate to see false hope on the face of a student. Usually.

Cooper nods and makes another note. "Are you sure you didn't stay at Bayview for a while after school let out? Visit anyone?"

"No. I just went to the beach and then home. I swear."

They fall silent. I can hear the buzzing of the bright lights. Their eyes lock and they stare at each other. Tyler breaks eye contact first, and looks at me, pleading in his eyes.

"Smoke crack?"

Tyler's head snaps back like a rubber band. "What?"

"I know you snort coke, unless you sell it all. I just want to know if you're as smart as the gangbangers in the ghetto or not. So are you smart enough to cook up crack?"

"I don't do drugs!"

Cooper opens up the folder on the table and begins tossing 8 by 8 glossies in front of Tyler. They show Ray's corpse from every angle.

"Aah!"

"So why'd you do it? Did he find out you were slinging rock and you just wanted to protect yourself?" Tyler's mouth opens and closes like a hooked grouper. "Did you and Jesse get so high you decided to murder Ray because he gave you bad grades?"

"I didn't kill him! I didn't even know he's dead!"

"I know you didn't kill him. Your hands aren't big enough. But I know Jesse did.

So was it your idea? Is Jesse just mindless muscle you get high and addicted so you can order him around for another fix?"

Tears roll one by one down my student's cheeks.

"Speak up motherfucker! Why'd you do it!"

"STOP!" I'm surprised someone with such small stature can project his voice so well. Cooper isn't phased. He has the strength of his convictions.

"Jesse already told us everything. Your only option is to confess. Maybe the Judge will take pity on you."

"I said stop! I want to see my mom! I'm not talking to you anymore!"

Cooper shrugs. "Your funeral, fuckface. You just missed your only chance at leniency." He storms out of the room, leaving the photos on the table. Tyler stares at them, his shoulders heaving.

I lay a hand on his back and rub gently. "Shh... it's okay. It's okay. I know you didn't do it."

"Mr. Kent, what am I going to do?"

"Tyler, I don't have much time. They're going to take me out of here soon. There's nothing I can tell this Detective to change his mind."

"Oh my God! This isn't happening!"

"Time to be strong. I can spend my few minutes here trying to make you feel better or I can give you advice on how to survive the near future."

Tyler sniffs.

"I have valuable advice. Do you want it?"

"I just... if I go to jail for life... I'm not scared of that as much as I'm afraid of..."

"Of what?"

My student finally looks me in the eyes. "I don't want to die a virgin."

Every young man's worst fear. And in this young man's face, actually understandable. "Let me tell you something. You know how in many primitive cultures they make virgin sacrifices to the Gods? Throw virgins into the volcano? You know why this is?"

"No..."

"It's because you're special. Virgins are worth more than normal people. You have a mystique about you. Sex is temporary, and afterward you're just another undersexed male. A dime a dozen. Virgins are a rare breed, appreciated and loved by all. Your virginity gives you power."

"Really?"

"Yes. You should tell the Judge what you told me. He'll understand that you're special." Tyler looks sick to his stomach but his hands aren't shaking anymore.

"Here's my advice on how to make it in prison. First, *don't give anyone your lunch*. It makes you look weak. Second, don't call anyone 'Chester'. Where you're going, respect and power are everything. If you hold yourself properly and look at people like you're not to be messed with, you won't be. But just in case someone disrespects you," I pick up one of the photos and fold it into a triangle, "you get a piece of newspaper, and you fold it like this. Over and over again. When it's small and pointed and thick, you scrape and sharpen it."

I hold the folded photo to my throat. "Go for the artery, here."

Standing up straight, I hear footsteps. A man in a suit launches himself into the room, trailed by Detective Cooper.

"This student's parents should have been informed immediately that their son has been taken from school!" Ah. This must be the lawyer.

"You don't think I did this, do you?" Tyler has his forehead on the table.

"-Don't say anything else, Tyler-"

"-Maybe he wants to say something else, you lawyer piece of-"

"No Tyler, I don't."

But if he asked me if I thought he deserved to be where he is right now, my unspoken reply would be "yes".

Don't defy the Principal.

"I bet the prints we found at the scene match these two," he says once we're outside the room. I follow him to interview room B. "We were close on the last one. You see how he cried? Sign of guilt. And he admitted that they were together. This next one will break. My senses as a Detective tell me this."

He places his hand on the door handle. Caresses it. "I smell blood in the water."

Inside, Jesse sits with his hands folded. He looks disinterested in his surroundings. Cooper plants himself in front of him and cracks his knuckles.

"Jesse. How are you?"

He doesn't speak, but just peers at me without blinking.

"Don't look at him. Look at me."

Jesse spits. It lands on my chin and hangs by a thread.

Cooper jumps up and pummels the table. "You motherfucker! You little shitstained condom! I will bury you! I'm going to put you away for life!" Jesse gives me the finger and Cooper the other one. I wipe the spittle off before it gets on my suit.

"I bet the glove fits. You will definitely try it on in court. We're done here." Jesse keeps the fingers directed at us as we leave.

Before the door closes I hear Jesse say, "It's not over."

Cooper slides his fingers backwards through slimy strings of hair as he paces the width of the hall. He reminds me of someone who had to leave the room in the middle of a blowjob.

"I have to say, Detective, I still can't believe my students could do such a thing. I was convinced they were good people."

He stops pacing. "Your opinion of them is biased because you're their Principal. Let me share something you need to hear. You live in a bubble. A safe, optimistic bubble. I know about the morbid ugly reality of the real world better than you; the reality regular folk avert their eyes and minds from because they need to believe this pretty picture of how life works in order to stay sane. The reality is: children are evil. Children are vicious. They have the jungle in them."

I didn't mean to vent his anger, but it's escaping from its pent-up container anyway. "They attack at the first sign of insecurity and pounce when they see weakness. They threaten, they harass, they instigate and exploit. They bully the small and smile and cackle while they do it. Worst of all, they group together simply to exclude those who don't fit in. They understand that it feels good to do bad things but haven't grown enough yet to feel empathy."

I want to ask him who teased him in high school. What I don't want to do is agree with him. It would be against everything I believe in. My children are pure. Everything I do is for them, absolutely everything. But when I think of Tyler and Jesse, I have to imagine they are no longer my students, or everything gets too complicated.

"As they grow, the concentrated evil in their body dilutes, spreads out. Eventually they become normal, decent adults like us. But until then, until they have the concept of right and wrong crammed into them year after year, they give as much thought to the consequences of violence as picking their nose."

"So you're sure they did it?"

"I'm positive. You were a big help to this case and I appreciate that. But you've done all you can. Tyler and Jesse are my responsibility now. You should go home and get some rest. Let the legal system do its work."

I nod. For some reason I get the urge to go back to Jesse's room. Why did he say it wasn't over? What does he know?

"Hello..." Cooper snaps his fingers in front of my face. "Did you hear me?"

"Sorry, what?"

"I said when the time comes, you'll need to testify. You'll need to tell the jury everything you told me. You're a vital part of this case, Adam. You know these boys. I trust you'll show the jury what twisted sadists they are."

I envision the courtroom in my head. The two accused stare at me next to their lawyers and parents. The audience is filled with people I know, and who know Tyler and Jesse. The judge looks at me solemnly. Do I have what it takes to seal the deal?

I nod. "I can do that."

If you're a Principal for long enough you can feel the collective psyche of your school like a pulse. I always have my finger on the pulse. Bayview's pulse right now is fluttering, weak, and scattered. The rhythm is off, rapid and uneven like one's heartbeat after a life-or-death scare. I can feel this from my office, even though everyone is gone. I touch the wall softly.

"Relax," I whisper. "Everything is alright." It's well past nine now. I should be heading home. On a whim, I decide to leave out the back of the school, cutting across the basketball courts. I'm almost outside before I can tell something's wrong. The frosted glass windows glow with a flickering orange-yellow light.

Lincoln High set the field on fire! The year's hopes and dreams of athletic redemption have been set ablaze!

I strike the door with the side of my hand and hurl myself through the opening.

Outside it is chilly with a slight breeze and utterly dark due to the absence of the moon. The football field is lit up by hundreds of tiny flames, but the inferno is too far off the ground to be burning grass. As I get closer, the scene resolves itself: the flames are candles held by silent people standing shoulder to shoulder. This could be a cult, or some elaborate attempt at intimidation by Lincoln High. They could be terrorists. The nearest person to me turns their head as I approach. It's Melinda Ruiz, one of the receptionists! She gives me a half-smile that doesn't reach her eyes. She stands next to Patrick Cena, sophomore, and Peter Volker, the shop teacher. These are all my students and employees! Am I too late? Have Tyler and Jesse actually incited a full-on uprising?

"What is the meaning of this?" I ask, trying to keep my voice even and free of inflection.

Melissa's glowing face twists up with uncertainty. "We're holding a candlelight vigil."

"But why here? Why now? And why so many people?"

"Is this a test? Some sort of joke?" She starts to sound angry, or maybe sad.

"No! Of course not!" I'm just asking questions. Why is everyone here so uptight?

"We're here because we're a community. When something like this happens, the community comes together."

All these people are here because of Raymond? Pathetic, infuriating, incompetent, friendless Raymond?

"Does this make you feel better?"

"No!" chorus voices joining in from the shadows.

"Then why are you doing this?"

Patrick walks up to me and hands me a tiny candle in a glass cup. "Because he should be alive to see this."

The wind picks up. All the candles dance in unison, highlighting tear tracks. I want to ask questions until I understand, but instead I fall silent and pretend to contemplate the candle, thinking profound thoughts. No matter what I ask, I'll never understand what everyone is doing here. And no matter how long they stand here, neither will they.

Death is like that.

8.

"If a student has trouble with the spelling of 'principle' versus 'Principal', tell them to always remember that the Principal is their P-A-L."

As someone involved in both the day-to-day minutiae and long term outlook of my school I face the dichotomy of idealism versus realism head on every day. People like Superintendent Burnside and my VP Chris Hasty are realists. By dint of their vocation, they have to be. And there's nothing wrong with that. When you deal with level upon level of strict bureaucracy or piles upon piles of financial, personnel and logistical paperwork you are shaped into a realistic mind set, focused on what is attainable and sustainable.

In the same way, my job shapes me. I take extra steps to avoid contact with mundane paperwork or supplicating myself to those above my pay grade. And there is nothing on school grounds outside my ability to change. Instead, I take a holistic approach. I have a vision, a desire, a plan. And I have the will and the authority to see them through. I become the change I wish to see in my school. After eight years here, I feel that an aerial view of Bayview High is akin to a portrait of my face or brain. It is an extension of my DNA.

I am an idealist, in the purest sense of the word.

Chris Hasty is waiting outside the main entrance as I walk up. I walk to and from school everyday. What I save in gas costs and various vehicle fees I can instead reinvest directly in the school. I give him a friendly wave. His eyes carry dark bags and his hair is a mess.

"My word, have you slept at all since the vigil? I myself slept like a baby last night. A person needs seven to eight hours to function effectively during the day, you know."

He makes a noise like he just took a tennis ball to the stomach. "I understand that it's important to be well rested but the added workload from the fundraising planning and committee meetings besides all the extra paperwork you delegate to me..."

I nod as he voices his complaints while not listening and instead focus on the school's façade. The glass double doors and matching full length windows are spotless, and above them the words BAYVIEW HIGH stand out brightly in unfaded paint matching the school's colors. Everything appears exactly the same as it was two days ago. As it should. Everyone here should understand that it's still business as usual. Nothing of consequence has happened. The school remains unblemished, inside and out.

Chris has apparently wrapped up. "I'm out here- besides, y'know, to say hi- because Tyler Dourden's parents are here."

"I see. They must be extremely grieved and ashamed of their son's behavior. Do they look grieved?"

"Actually, they just look angry."

"Hmmm. Thanks for telling me. I will see to this personally."

"I think I should be there too. I don't actually know very much about what happened, besides the basics. Maybe you could clue me in as to what you and the police have worked out about the murder?"

"All in good time, Chris. For now, just watch and take note of how to comfort parents in times of difficulty and fear. They just need someone to help them make sense of a world in which their son who they thought they knew brutally murdered another human being. To them it's like up is suddenly down and black is suddenly white."

When we enter the main office my desk ladies move to introduce me to Mr. and Mrs. Dourden, but they are already on their feet and in my face.

"We demand to speak with you. Out son is innocent!"

Tyler's father looks like he just got back from his cubicle. Tortoise shell glasses, short salt and pepper hair, collared shirt and chinos. His wife is attractive in a matronly way. She has on a patterned blouse that matches her eyes. Understandably he hasn't put on a tie and her pierced lobes are empty. Chris is right, they don't look like they've cried recently.

I make placating motions with my hands: palms halfway up and gently pushing outward. "I understand. Please, come into my office. This will be better in private."

Their voices are angry, but as we walk Mr. Dourden puts his arm around his wife as if to keep her from falling. She leans against him. If they weren't focusing all their anger on me, they'd have the hollow look of the shell-shocked.

The woman starts up before I can close the door behind us. "We've been at the police station all night. They only let us talk to Tyler for less than an hour. The Detectives said they're sending them to jail tomorrow!"

Mr. Dourden nods with his lips pursed. "They were arrested here for a crime they say happened here. You're responsible for all this. My boy did nothing wrong!"

I sit down behind my desk and motion for them to take a seat. They remain standing. "We've met before, once. Roger, right? And Cindy? Please, call me Adam."

"We will call you whatever we want. And we did meet before: at Tyler's valedictorian ceremony!"

"Ma'am, it may surprise you but many high-functioning drug users are impeccable students. The stress of maintaining it all is sometimes what drives them to drugs in the first place."

"Out son does not use drugs! Not at home, not anywhere!"

"Just because you didn't see it doesn't mean it wasn't happening. Children are very good at hiding such things from their parents. And though your son was a valedictorian, his grades have recently plummeted. No doubt he was too ashamed to tell you."

"We've seen his tests from Raymond's class. He aced every one!"

"Well, obviously he cheated and his grades were retroactively marked down. I would ask Mr. Paba to explain herself, but your son and his friend killed him."

Chris stutters. "Wh-what Mr. Kent means is that allegedly your son may have been involved in Mr. Paba's death. Principal Kent is not throwing accusations around willy nilly, he's just very distraught right now. He cared very deeply for Raymond."

Mrs. Dourden's rage emanates from her eyeballs. "We will sue. We will sue you for all you're worth."

I take a second to stare at her. "I don't think you want to take money away from all your son's classmates. Honestly, I think your legal fees would be better spent defending your son rather than suing me."

The rage leaves her eyes. Mostly. She stands up and wobbles on her feet. Her husband stands up slowly but doesn't falter. He puts his arm around her shoulders and whispers low in her ear. Her eyes get watery and she mutters something about it not being fair. They leave without another word and I can see that they're actually supporting each other.

Chris closes the door. The bags under his lids are darker than usual. He looks like a raccoon. That might be a gray hair at his temple but I can't be sure. "Adam? Would you like to have dinner with my wife and I? We can talk about this whole tragedy, plan how we should handle this aftermath? This huge Goddamn mess?"

I don't have time for this but I hide my impatience well. "I can't. Sorry."

He looks at the ground. "It would just be dinner. I've been working for you for a long time and you've never shared with me anything about your plans."

"Maybe tomorrow. We have work to do." I get on the intercom, "Hold my calls please. I am distraught." Really, I just need to get some air.

The children are still afraid as they walk the halls. Some are jumpy, some depressed. Walking the halls is no longer as relaxing as it was a week ago. As soon as I circle back to the office I get a whiff of a familiar expensive perfume. I claw my fingers despite myself.

Linda Chu, that sorry excuse for a Principal, is walking quickly towards me.

Oh no, I know that look.

I put up my hands, but it's too late, and she hugs me anyway and holds it for far too long. "I'm so sorry! So, so sorry!"

"For what?"

That gets her off me fast. "What?"

"What are you sorry for? I have not an inkling of what you mean."

For the first time I see Chu get angry. "The murder that happened on your campus! Your students' incarceration!"

"That's none of your concern. Go back to your awful school and continue to rake in your private school blood money." It feels wonderful to talk to her like this, without pretense.

Chu can only stutter. Or stammer. I knew she was a stutterer. Then she takes a breath and goes from angry to cold. "This wouldn't have happened if you didn't stifle your students' individuality and creativity at every opportunity."

"I don't do that."

"Yes you do. That newsletter? I think it's driving you nuts. Are Tyler and Jesse the ones who wrote it?"

She has no proof. It's an obvious bluff. "You are the last one I'd expect to accuse a grief-stricken Principal of murder. Unprofessional to the extreme. Plus, you wouldn't know 'nuts' if you saw it." Time to twist the knife and throw salt. Seven years ago, one of her golden couples didn't make it to graduation.

"At least my golden couple knows enough to drive carefully through the Ash Street intersection. You're the one who's guilty of murder. It's your job to educate your kids. Don't throw stones."

No reaction, just ice. I'm almost impressed. "I knew you were nuts. I will destroy you." Ah well, one more person to add to my list of enemies.

Oh wait, she was already on the list.

"Not if I destroy you first. Keep on shooting up your receivers with steroids. They'll need it. In every sport, in every debate, my students will crush yours. I will spend all my time reducing your school to a worse condition than Central High. You're a private school. Parents can vote with their feet and the withdrawal of their deposit from the bank of Linda."

Chu can't take it anymore and spins around, unable to handle the cold hard truth. I'm shocked. She lasted longer than I thought. And she discreetly flips me the bird before she leaves my sight. I can't help but respect her a smidgen for that. I think I like this unprofessional version of her. Time to patrol the grounds some more and clear my head. I should work on The Principal's Guide to Success right now but I'm too restless to sit still. Writing can wait.

Outside the band room I can hear the faint sounds of the choir through the closed door. They sing like angels. I drink it in, the sadness saturating the song only making it more arresting. I thought this was arranged as a happy song, though.

Steps behind me. I look back to say hello, hopefully provide some comfort with my cheerfulness. It's Blake Hoffman, holding a leash that dangles loosely from his girlfriend's neck to the floor to his hand. Am I hallucinating?

"What in Jehova's name are you doing?"

Caitlin speaks up: "It was my idea. It shows that I belong to him and no one else can have me." Blake nods and sniffs snot. Another sickness spreading? "And he's mine. That's why he's wearing the ring."

"He's treating you like an animal. A dog. Do you know the technical term for a female dog? I won't say it, but it's what I see when I look at you two."

"Maybe I am his bitch. Maybe I like it. And when we're not at school, who do you think wears the collar?" Her posture screams pure defiance. I haven't seen this in many years.

Steve Ortiz, the best quarterback I've ever had, strides by without looking. "We will be arranging for a wardrobe change," I quickly blurt. "Steve! Steve!"

He stops, and his face at least is honestly respectful. "Yes Mr. Kent?"

"Are you okay? How are you feeling? Do you want to talk about it with me? Or one of the counselors?"

"Thank you, but I'm fine. I didn't really like Mr. Paba. I think all this mourning stuff is... bullshit," he grins. "And don't worry. It won't affect my spiral. And our defensive line *hated* him." Music to my ears. Removing Mr. Paba from this planet was the best thing that happened to this school in recent memory. I pat Steve on the back and send him on his way. Soon every one of my students will be like Steve.

I heard the discordant sound of a parakeet from somewhere outside. Wild urban parakeet mating calls are loud and disruptive to learning. Where is it?

Entering the quad I see litter spread across the concrete. I relish picking it up and throwing it in the trash can where it belongs. It feels so gratifying right now that I'm not even angry. But... something is wrong. Very wrong. I stare at the crumpled paper in my hand. It trembles. I unfold it slowly. Exact same letterhead. Exact same format. Exact same subversive voice. The headline drives nails into my skull. The headline says INNOCENT. It has large black and white photos of Jesse and Tyler.

One glance and I throw it away. Whomever wrote it doesn't know the truth; they are merely guessing. But they are still out there.

The headline screams at me from the garbage. Even as I leave at the end of the day, it doesn't get any quieter.

That night I walk to Jesse's house because I sold my car long ago. Running my hand on the slumping fence, I see peeling paint, a rotting leaf-covered roof, a cracked window, and empty beer cans and broken glass and cigarette butts scattered about the yard. When I knock on the chipped front door, a low voice says "What?"

"It's Principal Kent, sir. I'd like to talk to you about your son." I take the ensuing silence as consent and step inside.

The air is hazed with cigarette smoke. Mike Corvall doesn't look up, just uses a butt to light a new cigarette before flicking it onto an overflowing clay ashtray. His shirt has multiple small burns. There's a small patch of black mold on the kitchen wall and the smell of dog feces. He stares at the news on the glowing television screen. A large Bayview championship ring adorns the ring finger of his smoking hand. It's decades old.

"Sir, I'd just like to convey how sorry I am that your son had to be arrested. I'm convinced of his innocence, and I will fight tooth and nail to make sure he is released and the charges are dropped. My school's safety is in doubt, and I feel increasing shame everyday. I'm trying to make my students feel safe again. But they don't. I can't understand what you're going through, but I would like to extend to you any help I can offer."

Mike cracks open a beer and sucks off the foam. "Stop babbling."

I do.

"I always knew Jesse was a piece of shit. And I knew he's been doing drugs. His mother was a cunt and a cokehead, and no matter how much discipline I used, he kept mouthing off just like she did. If he played a sport he would have learned some discipline, earned my respect. He doesn't know the meaning of hard work. He never will." He chugs the beer in seconds; crushes it in one hand. He has large, calloused hands.

"Where do you work?" I ask, unable to think of what to say next.

He looks away from the TV for the first time. Ash falls onto his protruding gut. His eyes are very red. From lack of sleep? No. Marijuana? Methamphetamine? Or from crying, maybe. Staring at a screen for the whole day? He has the thousand-yard stare. He's had it for a while, not just for the last week.

"You took him out of my life. That's the one thing I wanted in life but couldn't do.

Don't expect me to thank you. Now get... out... of... my... house."

There's no logic to this, but I desire nothing more than to beat him into an unconscious twisted lump on the dirty floor. I don't know if I could beat this man in a fight, and I say that about very few men. And he poses no threat to my job. But I want to rip out his trachea and then feed it to him.

He turns his stare at the screen again. "If you want to get me a beer before you leave it's in the icebox."

"Will you visit-"

"Now," he says. Not yelling, not growling. I have to leave.

Outside the yard and the fence I kneel in the middle of the street and punch the asphalt until my hands are wet and numb and I can breathe again. For a brief moment, I don't care about anything. Not even my school.

9.

"Question every assumption you make about each one of your students on a daily basis."

Strips of shadow from the bars over the windows. Knife in hand, dripping red. I silently leave bloody bare footprints on the institutional floor. A man's back is to me, inviting the blade. His face is to the television. Static. I lift and thrust down. He falls to the ground, thick white smoke rising from the wound, and a blood flecked football rolls between my feet.

I snap from the daydream to reality with a realization that spreads warmth throughout my body. Tomorrow night is the big game. Bayview versus Lincoln. Good against evil. Triumph over adversity. Redemption. The restoration of peace to the minds of my students. After our victory, we can go back to the way things were. I know this because I am the Principal. I need to gaze upon out mascot and its extinct jaws.

Soon I am pondering the Tasmanian Tiger's eyes. Pure ferocity. It's jaws speak of punishment to those who steal undeserved victories. I slowly stroke the fur while pressing my cheek to its underbelly. When I step back I see a couple students staring at me, their thoughts hidden. I raise a hand in acknowledgement. "I may be taking the game tomorrow a little seriously. Can you blame me?" After hesitating, they shake their heads. "Thank you. I needed to know that you understand. Please support the team with your lustful war cries." They hesitate, then nod, and then slowly back away.

I feel as if I am balancing on a small round rock. Fifteen feet to the front office, and it takes me a whole minute to get there. My office ladies look up and me and smile as I enter. At least they are unchanged. They do so much for this school. They handle attendance issues, deal with irate parents, handle every student that breaks the dress code, and do it all with a complete lack of visible emotion. Every parent and student that enters here leaves with a newfound respect for the institution's efficient equality. I greet each of the five students sitting in the perimeter waiting chairs by first name. One actually smiles. Suddenly I feel a strong physical need to search some lockers.

Naturally I start with Brandon Nelson's. Digging around through the books and hats and debris I find a history textbook. When I lift it, it feels light. Did he hollow out a schoolbook? Vandalizing school property is certainly his style, after all.

I open it up and I find a tiny baggie of white powder. It takes my breath away.

I told him what would happen if I found drugs in his locker again. And *cocaine*? He is endangering the lives of my students just as if he walked onto campus with a loaded handgun. Time to remove this filthy waste of oxygen from my school now. I don't want to pass him off onto another Principal, but he is beyond my help. I know exactly which class he is in. I have most if not all of my students' schedules memorized. I will take care of this in twenty minutes flat. I won't even take the time to savor it. Strictly business.

When I enter Mr. Holt's biology class Brandon's face twists into its usual sneer. I grab him by the wrist (not too hard, but enough to convey my seriousness) and take him out of class. He shakes my hand off. I smile at him. I've never smiled at him before and it terrifies him. We walk all the way to the corner of chain link fence that marks the northeastern border of my school- deserted as it always is during fourth period- and then I order him to sit on the closest bench.

"You crossed the line. Your time here is over. I won't even talk to your parents. I'm kicking you out of Bayview now and you can explain the situation to them yourself." His face says that the joy he feels at leaving this school is outweighed by the dread of revealing to his parents what a soulless lump of mud he is. I toss the baggie in the air. Out of reflex he reaches up and grabs it, and meanwhile I reach into his jacket pocket and extract his cell phone.

"No!"

I need to work my way up the supply chain or else it will be another student who brings this poison into my school. Holding up a hand but not touching him, I keep him cornered and helpless. He drops the coke.

"Who is it? Is it 'Matt'? or 'Skinny'? Maybe 'Troy'? Or maybe-" A name catches my eye and won't let go. " 'Wesley P'? Wes Petersen? Same Wes that used to be a student here? What are you doing with Wes's number?"

Silence. When I look in Brandon's face I feel myself sinking into a cold hole. He knows I know and he can't help but look guilty.

"Wes is supplying you? A former student? He was a valedictorian!" Nothing makes sense anymore. I don't even know how long it's been since things did. When was my school normal?

I pick up the coke and have trouble straightening back up. The heavy past hangs on my back. Brandon's face has no color. He knows I could break his nose right now and get away with it. I still have total power on this campus.

"Next time you pick up from Wes, you call me with the time and location. You have two weeks. If you don't...." I am at a loss. Specific threats may not have an effect. "If you don't I will punish you in ways you haven't dreamt of in your darkest nightmares."

I pull away. He slumps to the floor once I am at a distance, sobbing perhaps. The only thing that's heavier than the weight on my shoulders is the poison in my pocket.

Chris Hasty waves me down in the four way C-Wing/D-wing intersection. "Adam, I'm extremely busy right now with all the parents coming in and I need you to take care of some situations. Please. If you're not busy. I need you on this."

I welcome this news. I need distractions and lots of them. I need to do some good for this school, truly good, that can't be complicated with morality. I need to do my job. It's all I want to do for the rest of my life. "Yes Chris. I'll take care of everything. Just keep placating the parents until this thing blows over."

For some reason Chris flinches when I say the last two words. "Great. Excellent. Jasmine O'Connell passed out in Vicky Cross's biology class. It's probably from abusing cough syrup. And apparently all of the furniture in Mr. Davidson's English class is stuck to the ceiling. He's having a minor nervous breakdown."

Yes. Problems that can be solved. Chances to prove that I am still the best Principal this school has ever had. Opportunities to show that there's nothing I can't fix. Nothing.

Jasmine's incident is more pressing. I hustle as fast as I can without running and maybe because I'm hurrying and obviously on my way to make things better for everyone or maybe because enough time has passed that the psychological pain of Raymond's death is gone every individual smiles at me as I blow past.

I take the time to knock before I push into the classroom. Everyone- even the teacher- are ignoring Jasmine, who is facedown in her own vomit but breathing. I dig deep into my brain to find knowledge of Jasmine's personality and character. I realize that about half the time I've seen her in class she sits with her eyes half closed, nodding off. I thought she was tired from studying since her grades were so exemplary! Why couldn't I see past that deep enough?

"Please do not be alarmed! I will leave no child behind! I can fix everything!" Everyone looks at me and then goes back to messing around. I realize that no one here looks afraid or sad anymore. It's just young people enjoying twenty minutes of unexpected... freedom? I'm so glad at this that I don't feel distressed in the least that valuable time is being wasted. I just want to hear genuine enjoyment again.

I gently bring Jasmine to her feet and support her. She can somewhat stand. She is also drooling on my tie.

Without warning the anger comes back. Someone is still out there, ready to destroy everything good in my life. But I don't drop Jasmine. In fact, I lift her higher up and place her head on my shoulder. And when she vomits again it's almost the high point of my day. After I leave her in a nurse's professional care and make a mental note to check up on Jasmine every day I walk to Mr. Davidson's class.

The scene is surreal. Every single desk and chair stuck upside down on the ceiling. Except for Mr. Davidson's desk, which I guess was too heavy to lift. He has a haunted look in his eyes. The students, all standing, look at me with innocence. If any of these students are responsible for this, they hide it well.

"I don't understand!" Mr. Davidson wails. "Just like in my dreams! How is this possible?"

"Why don't you take a ten, Bill? Focus on your breathing. I see this too. You are not dreaming." Bill shudders and hurriedly exits.

I stare around the class. Everyone has heard of how seriously I loathe class time that is not spent learning. But they don't look afraid. The students seem to be waiting for a reaction, a reaction that confirms the vile rumors perpetuated by the Gazette. I don't smile- that would be too much- but I'm sure my posture communicates that I am not angry. "I don't want to know who did this. I don't care about the Who. I want to know the How. Anyone who explains how this was accomplished will not be punished. In fact, they will be rewarded with a free Bayview Tasmanian Tiger snapback baseball cap, now available for purchase in the student store at a reduced price."

Silence, then Tristen Dent shrugs up his shoulders and raises his hand. "I don't know if this is true or not," he looks around to make sure no one wants him to shut up, "but I heard that thirty or forty years ago some airplanes were held together in spots with... I guess it's called aviation tape? And this stuff is really strong. So maybe someone's dad had some that he forgot about." He looks down for a moment, thinking. "Maybe we want Mr. Davidson to listen to us instead of talking for the whole period. Like, actually answer our questions, you know?"

"This is certainly a strange way to go about changing Mr. Davidson's behavior. But I do not necessarily disapprove. Just come to me directly next time, alright? Scooter is going to have a hard time cleaning this up. Any suggestions?"

Amy Hood speaks in what could only be called a squeak. "Maybe hydrochloric acid? There's a lot in the class across the hall."

Never would have expected Amy to be the mastermind. Twice today I have been surprised by my students. This is one reason that I love them all. The new developments. The depth of their intelligence. They keep getting smarter!

After final period ends, sitting alone on the front steps, I take stock of the day. Maybe my indefatigable positivity is starting to bring my students back around. Best case scenario, they're starting to realize how much better everyone is without Raymond or Tyler or Jesse in their lives. The big game is tomorrow, and maybe victory isn't quite as important as the peace it will bring.

Cigarette smoke.

"Adaaaaam!" The oily voice matches the face. "Good to see ya!" Cooper is wearing what appears to be the same clothing that he was wearing a week ago. He smells worse, too. Can't he afford more than one suit?

I instantly put on a friendly façade. "Detective! It is very good to see you! I'm sorry, but could you please put out your cigarette? School's out, but it's still against the law."

He squints. "Goddamn you're a tightass," he grumbles before he stomps it into the cement. "I came to tell you about some recent developments."

"Excellent! Are Tyler and Jesse doing okay? Are they healthy? Safe?"

"Fuck if I know. Those scummy bastards can die in jail for all I care. In my opinion that would be true justice. If it were up to me they'd be getting injected with the lethal stuff right now.

"I came to tell you what the CSI's told me. Lazy motherfuckers finally did their jobs." He examines my face, gauging my response as runs his hands through his hair. It stands up with its own natural wax.

"Please, Detective. The more I know, the more I can help you solve this mystery."

"Oh, no mystery. They did it." He starts hacking until a congealed yellow wad rockets from his mouth and lands on my left shoe. "Ahhh. Anyway, the CSI's report backs up your story completely. Except they found some epithelial cells inside one of the gloves. You know what epithelial cells are?"

Yes I do. I've thought about them a lot since Raymond's removal. "Skin cells."

He punches my shoulder. "We got a fuckin' smart guy over here! Right. The DNA in these tiny little pieces of skin don't match Tyler or Jesse. Or Raymond. They won't tell me where they got the gloves, and the little pricks' lawyer says those little pricks don't know who the gloves belong to. It's irritating as the inside of a dry pussy, that's for sure." He starts picking behind a molar with his finger.

"I want you to find those responsible for this murder, but I am also glad that my students may not be guilty."

"What? What the *fuck* are you saying?" He's using the same voice he used on my students. It's not unnerving me in the least. "You told me they were bad students. You pointed them out to me. It's because of you I found the drugs and the blood," he says, his voice becoming shrill. "You hate those little demons at much as I do! Don't lie!"

But I can't lie because I'm no longer sure of the truth. I don't know if I've ever been unable to lie while I've been in control of Bayview.

"Justice must be done. If I need to testify, I will tell the jury exactly what I told you."

Detective Cooper eyeballs my face. "Good. And you better believe you will testify! Physical evidence might no longer contribute to making our case. The jury hears about the skin cells and that's reasonable shitcake doubt right there. I think I can call in some favors and keep the DNA stuff out of the courtroom but the whole case is now hinging on your testimony. If you don't demonstrate to the jury that these shitdick kids are hardcore murderous cokeheads, they walk. And then they're out on the street, free to kill again. You could be next. You probably *will* be next."

He coughs lung snot onto his own shoe this time. "Comprende?"

I comprehend that Tyler and Jesse must stay locked up forever. The school is just now coming under my control again. Everyone is getting happy again. Everyone is realizing that they are safe. I can't have Tyler or Jesse come back to bring this school down around my feet. Once I take care of the Gazette once and for all, once all those guilty are eliminated with prejudice, then the world will be as it should. When I testify, only the choicest lies will leave my lips.

"Yes. You don't need to worry about me. Just keep doing your job and I'll do mine."

"That's what I like to hear! Remember, it's our only shot." Yellow teeth twist into

59

a grin.

Did he say "our" only shot? Did he just group us together as if we're anything alike? I keep my ties spotless!

He pulls out a crumpled pack and shakes out a bent cigarette before he tosses the pack on the ground. He slurs with it dangling between his lips: "Keep this in mind, Mr. Principal: a majority of the shitty kids at this school- and all of them are shitty, believe me- will grow up into shitty adults living fat on the taxes of employed people like us. You need to understand this. It will make you a better Principal.

"Think of what we're doing as preventative maintenance. Ounce of motherfucking prevention, am I right?" A click of his metal lighter, and then a cloud of rank smoke makes my eyes water.

I have to relax my jaw and unclench my teeth before I say, "I don't tell you how to do your job. Please extend to me the same courtesy."

He grins again. "You know I'm all about courtesy."

Then he finally leaves, his unique odor trailing behind him. The back of his coat is as disgusting as the front. I don't think this is because he spends all of his time totally focused on the job. That can't be true. It doesn't take that much time to keep my clothes clean. I feel something odd deep down inside.

Fear?

It's very late. I'm still at the school. In a handicapped stall in fact, kneeling over the closed toilet lid. I have a thick line of white powder in front of me, whiter even than the toilet itself. Maybe because of the fluorescent light. I'd like to think my toilets are whiter than this dried pile of venom. It's most definitely been stepped on. With what, baby laxative? Baking powder? Meth? Drain cleaner? Maybe Wes is trying to get at me through Brandon and it's a hot shot.

This is exactly what my enemies want. This isn't what I want. I'm clean. I'm clean. I'm clean. The empty baggie sits close by with some residue still inside. I scrape it out and then tap a line onto the porcelain with my ID card. I know the sound well. I'm getting a rush just hearing it. But not enough of one. Not enough to make me sure of myself again. Not enough to feel like a good person.

I lean down, just for a closer look, but halt when I hear doors slam and an engine roar out front. Who is that? No one ever comes here at night, not since I found some burglars in the act long ago and righteously disposed of them.

The faster I sprint, the more nausea I feel. I told Scooter I'd lock up before I left. How long have I been cutting those lines? I be in the monitor room! After skidding to a stop I appraise the glass double front doors. One is ajar so slightly I almost can't see it. I smell fresh paint.

My Tasmanian Tiger is completely black. They must have used a whole can; the fumes are almost visible. She's soaked and ruined. They didn't get any on the walls or the tiles or the trophy case, but that makes it worse. The precision shows that this was not a split second decision. This was planned, meant to send a blow directly to the school's heart.

"I'm sorry," I whisper. "I should never have thought that victory wasn't the most important thing in this world." It replies with either a silent, agonized scream or a roar of defiance.

One foot in front of the other, in front of the other, and I am inside my office. I dial Chris's number.

"Who is this?" It's Chris's wife.

"This is the Principal. Put Chris on."

Dead silence.

"Please. It's very urgent. I need his help." Still no response, but also no dial tone. What is this woman's problem? Does she not understand that this mascot is more important than anything going on in her life right now?

60

I'm ready to break the receiver against my desk when I hear Chris's voice. He sounds tired, angry, and oddly concerned. "It's almost one. I have kids, Adam. I need sleep. What could possibly be going on?"

"They did it. The Lincoln High players. Chu. The Gazetters. They did it."

"You need to slow down. What do you mean? Who did what?"

"Principal Chu. Or the Gazette writers. They hired a proxy force- professional infiltrators. They defiled the mascot. They ruined it. I have to get rid of it. And the game is tomorrow!" I scream.

Chris yawns, and even though I know he is just tired it sounds like he does not care in the least. "I'm sorry about the mascot. That's very sad and unfortunate. But think about this for a second: they could have broken the doors. They could have destroyed a lot more stuff. Was it just the mascot?"

"Just the mascot? What do you mean *just* the mascot? Yes they did, but don't you see? It's a message! We were attacked by experts, hired by Chu to end this rivalry once and for-"

"Principal Chu did not hire a proxy force. It was a couple football players, probably drunk, having some fun. The mascot was getting old, Adam. It had sentimental value, sure, but we can afford a new one. A plastic one without the fake fur, cheap-looking, so it's not even worth vandalizing. There is no conspiracy. There are no connections. It's just you and how you react.

"Get some sleep. It'll all be put into perspective in the morning. I'll see you then, boss." Dial tone.

Words won't come out, just dry choking. If Chris doesn't understand, no one will. It's me against the world. I reach under the desk and feel the axe's reassuring weight. The smoothness of the handle speaks to me.

Revenge.

Lincoln High is miles away but when I get there I'm not sweating. The axe feels almost weightless. I look up at the dolphin above the scoreboard. Big stupid grin. Taunting. Asking for dismemberment and then the scattering of the chunks throughout the school, the head placed neatly on Chu's desk for her to see when she opens the door, the axe buried neatly in her chair.

"Is this how you solve all your problems, Mister Principal? Will you do this to one of your students next time?"

My neck snaps around, but I can't see anyone. I can't see anything but an empty field lit by pools of yellow-orange light. Did the dolphin just speak to me?

"No! This is not how I solve my problems, not anymore! Raymond was the last! I swear!"

"Prove it."

I realize it's only me talking to myself. My hands are still scabbed over. Once I start punching the ground I can't stop until the feelings go away, and by then my hands will be done. For good.

So I walk back to what used to be my sanctuary, grab the only mascot I've ever known, and carry it all the way back to that evil dolphin.

The Tiger still reeks of paint fumes and it goes up like a match.

It's almost getting light out so I don't stay to watch it burn, but if it catches the building on fire and takes the whole disgusting school down, so be it.

I don't remember walking back to Bayview the second time but I'm back in the spacious bathroom stall dripping sweat onto the toilet. "It's this, or my hands, or Lincoln High. One is going away for good."

And I choose the drugs and the second I do the school is my sanctuary again. Guess I'm staying up late tonight.

10.

I feel great. Extremely awake, alert, and yet relaxed. I can tell that others see the gleam in my eye and are cheered by it. My feet are light, and they don't walk or stride so much as dance. The air is sweet. The past is so far gone I can't even see it on the distant horizon behind me where the restless dead writhe and rot. The birds are chirping directly to me. I love everyone so much. I haven't thought about the impossible continued existence of the gazette since I left the handicapped stall last night.

"Hey mister Ken, where's the mascot?" Shrug.

"What happened to the stuffed animal you're always talking to?" Dunno.

"It's the big game, Principal Kent! Did someone steal our Tiger?" Of course not.

"The big girl's gone!" Just getting cleaned.

Chris is talking low to Mr. Gutierrez the department head. They don't see me, and I relish placing an arm around each of their shoulders. "Gentlemen! Beautiful day for a football game, no?"

Gutierrez seems to choke off a scream. Good man. I like a teacher bringing such energy to their workplace this early in the morning. "Hi! I gotta... I gotta go! Chris we'll talk later!"

"Where's the fire, ha ha! Chris, I'm sorry I woke you up last night. Totally unprofessional of me. I apologize." He ends the matter with a gesture. "Give me some news! Good, bad, whatever. What's the word on the street?"

Our eyes lock. He takes a deep breath. "Sir, you haven't looked at the paperwork I've been leaving on your desk for I don't know how long. If you had, you'd be very concerned about the school's financial situation."

I despise anything that has to do with money, preferring to focus on individual students and the overall physical environment of my school. But right now I'd like nothing better than to help Chris solve the school's money problems. "What's the financial situation? What's the big problem?"

"We have no money. Absolutely no money. If the anonymous donations have stopped for good, we'll be operating at a loss next month."

It's like a foreign language. "What would be the consequences?"

"Cutting positions. Cutting sports and clubs. Cutting bus routes. Larger classes, less teachers, lower salaries. Eventually we'll be reusing out of date books and cutting book purchases for the library. We may even have to alter the free and reduced lunch system."

All of a sudden I need to do another line. "We'll need to start doing these things... next month?"

"Yes, or else we'll start to lose federal and state funding. Closing the school is a very real possibility."

"How is this possible? We get millions of dollars in funding annually! We actually keep our students in their seats!"

"The state is bankrupt. Actually the whole country... the whole world is going bankrupt. The banks overleveraged themselves as usual, and the only method they can think of to fix the situation is to go deeper into debt. A vicious cycle, they call it. Not only is there less money to go around, but everything is more expensive. Pardon my language, but it's all fucked."

"And my students pay the price." The school's been through rough times before. I've had to fire teachers and administrators, make sacrifices and hard decisions. The school could close? The school's never been in danger of closing. I'll go to the governor's office and personally force him to write Bayview a check at gunpoint before I allow them to take away everything I live for.

"Leave it to me, loyal VP. I mean, keep doing whatever it is you do, you know, paperwork-wise. But don't stress too much about the school's future. As long as I draw breath, Bayview's doors will remain open and scratch-free!"

My co-worker- no, my friend- smiles for the first time in a long time. "Sure thing, Adam. If anyone can pull a solution to this out of thin air, it's you," he says as he does his usual nervous habit of running his fingers through his hair. So he's happy now, but still stressed. That's a start. I can fix people's problems all day, without even trying.

"Also," he adds, "there's another meeting of the department heads right now. I can't moderate this time, there's some sort of issue at Lincoln High right now, something about their parking lot, and I need to make sure that they're still going to show up-"

"And be soundly defeated."

"-and be defeated so bad they cry on the bus ride back, yes. Could you please attend the meeting and make sure all the various departments remove their hands from each others' throats?"

I could do that while somnambulating. I can solve the budget issue mentally at the same time I placate my highly positioned employees. "With pleasure Chris. Thanks for being you." A pat on the back, a knowing smile, and I'm off.

Within five minutes I'm at the head of the table in conference room A, already bored out of my skull. All these people just need to vent at their boss, and all I have to do is nod and act like I'm listening and will do exactly what they ask me to do. Which I won't, because it would cost money the school apparently doesn't have. What can I do to get the school more money? Some sort of fundraiser? Increase ticket prices? Maybe-

"I need to speak about a matter that will not wait." Mrs. Koont's voice cuts through my productive musings like a sword through someone's neck.

"Yes, Mrs. Koont?" She's almost seventy, tenured, and completely oblivious to everything but her lesson plan. Totally benign. This can be taken care of right now.

"My male students are no longer paying attention to me in class. At all. Normally they are completely attentive and open to learning. Now only one or two are making eye contact with me at a time."

Shocking. "You have total control over the lesson plan, Mrs. Koont. You've been teaching far longer than I've been here. I'm sure you can find some way to get the students interested in your class again."

"It's the male students only. And this is being caused by something new, something I've never seen before in all my years of teaching."

Wait a minute... this can't be about what I think it's about. Can it?

"It's the underwear the females are wearing. These... thongs." She says the word like it sours her tongue.

"I doubt that's the reason the boys seem distracted. You just need to change your teaching strategy."

"No I don't! I don't need to do that at all. All these harlots need to do is let their pants slide down an inch and it draws the males' eyes like some sort of major car accident! Their eyes should be on me for the entire duration of the class, not on their classmates' posteriors! We need to institute school-wide changes now!"

"This isn't covered in the dress code-"

"Section 18.3: 'Any article of clothing or lack thereof that is deemed inappropriate or detrimental to the learning environment must be changed for more appropriate dress immediately or suspension is required!'" I forgot that Mrs. Koont quotes sections of the dress code like passages from the Bible.

"What would you have me do? They're not visible most of the time, so the authorities have no way of knowing who should be sent to the office for a change of clothes."

"It's simple. Undergarment checks."

What? "Undergarment... checks?"

"Yes. It's actually very simple. If someone is suspected of displaying any of the many varieties of inappropriate, distracting undergarments an official member of the administration must verify the truth of this claim. If verified, the student must change immediately or be suspended." I can't believe what I'm hearing. Why does this woman care so much about my students' personal dressing choices?

"Maybe we could require school uniforms, maybe. But the students would never approve, and the time and effort implementing such legislation would be immense."

"Uniforms are external! It wouldn't solve the problem. And the costs of my solution are very low. One person, a few minutes a day, and the students' attention deficit problems are healed."

"Their parents would never approve."

"It's not the parents' decision to make. Or the students' decision. Or your decision. It is the decision of this entire room and this room alone that becomes law. We can put it to a vote."

I love Democracy as much as the next person, but I will never allow these simpletons any control over my students' lives. I am the only one with that power. "And if I disagree with your decision and veto it?"

Mrs. Koont's eyes narrow until they are almost completely closed. "Those of us with tenure are already in unanimous agreement. The distraction issue has become critical and widespread. If you do not comply with the majority decision of those assembled, we will challenge you at every future opportunity. You can't afford to fire us, Mr. Kent. We aren't going *anywhere*."

I give Chris the signal to call my phone so I can make a quick exit and let him sort out this mess. However, Chris is not here. I shouldn't need him for this, but I do.

One last attempt at reason. "How can we be sure that the person doing the checks can be trusted? How can we be sure that this person, male or female, is not taking the opportunity to fondle and molest our innocent young girls? Do you not see the immorality of what you are suggesting?"

She snorts. "If they are making such obscene dress choices, they are hardly 'innocent' or 'young'. And the process will be videotaped and reviewed by a third party. Any untoward behavior on the part of the inspector will result in immediate dismissal."

That is a small comfort. Where is Chris? Where did this sudden burst of audacity and mettle come from? What is this old withered woman's problem? "And who would you possibly choose for to grant this impossible responsibility to?"

"I leave that *entirely* in your hands."

An even smaller comfort. "It appears I have no choice. I will admit I feel like I've been ambushed."

I wish her laugh was the actually the death rattle it sounded like. "You can't play both sides against the middle anymore, Principal. You haven't addressed any of what we've brought up for years. This school used to care about its employees as much as its students. Well, it's time for things to go back to the way things were."

I feel a chill at her last words. "All in favor?" Will they all take her side?

They all do.

I can't stand to be here any longer. I should never have come in here. "I will start the paperwork immediately then." And I will make sure it stays in paperwork limbo until that old crone finally dies and turns to dust. "Meeting adjourned."

"But we haven't all had a chance to speak yet," says Mr. Gutierrez.

"The meeting is adjourned. Now." These backstabbing devils have won a temporary victory, but even with triumph coursing through their veins they know not to push their luck. I make personal, nonverbal threats with each formerly respectable adult as I pass. I don't say 'this isn't over'. They know.

I have a massive storm cloud floating over my head, crackling with lightning. I'm so enraged I almost pass by the student store without a second glance. But I am the

Principal. Even after a massive setback I am already on the lookout for the next positive step I can take to maintain Bayview's perfection. I haven't forgotten Chris's words. Insurmountable budget problems? I'll create a path to budget surplus before the big game tonight!

I never noticed how much bare space there was in the student store. Some hats and shirts, various small pins to place on jackets and backpacks, and a few scrunchies for some reason. It's currently staffed by Thomas DuPlont, a 3.9 GPA junior. "Hi Mr. Kent!" he chirps.

"Does this place seem a little empty to you, Thomas?"

"Yeah, but there aren't usually kids in here until lunch."

"No, I mean merchandise wise. Do you think we're selling enough things?"

Thomas ponders this. "I don't know, Mr. Kent. How much is enough?"

"Not this, that's for sure. Let me tell you, I just had a revelation. Soon, in addition to hats and shirts we will be selling personalized footballs, baseballs, and basketballs. Foam fingers. Hats in all colors and styles and sizes. Customized, expensive bobbleheads in the likeness of our admirable sportsmen. Autographed 12 by 12 glossies. And candy, lots of candy. Every square inch of this room will display items that students not only want to purchase, but items every student unconsciously *needs* to purchase."

Looking around the room, Thomas looks not quite convinced. "That would probably cost a lot."

"Yes it will. And it will earn even more." I give him a thumbs up. "I hope you're experienced enough at this position to handle a lunch period of non stop monetary transactions!"

A smile of enthusiasm and perhaps a bit of fear. "You know it!"

That was just the thing to wash the bad taste out of my mouth. Budget surplus by the end of the year, guaranteed. I want to tell Chris the good news, but he's still gone. Nagging thoughts of the Gazette begin to wiggle their way into the center of my brain. Who's writing it now? Why hasn't there been a new issue since the one proclaiming Tyler and Jesse's innocence? How many have read it? How many believe its lies?

"Princpal Kent? Hey!" A young freshman's voice.

I snap to. "Hello Casey. Excited for the big game tonight?"

"Yeah, of course. I'm supposed to go to your office right now."

Students get sent to my office for many reasons, some more serious than others. "Thanks for being honest with me. And why have you been sent to my office?"

"I got voted out."

"You got voted out? What does that mean?"

He shrugs his shoulders under his bulky sweater which conspicuously lacks Bayview's colors or logo. "We got a sub today. She asked everyone who should leave the class, and they voted me out. I don't really mind, that b... lady doesn't know the material anyway."

This will not stand. I love Democracy as much as the next red-blooded American, but today it seems that Democracy's perverted cousin is destroying this school from the inside out. Isn't the Gazette enough? Why are there so many threats to this school all of a sudden?

I know students like to give subs a hard time, but that's no excuse for giving students the authority to remove fellow classmates from the room. I need an explanation for this now. "Thank you for bringing this to my attention. You may patrol the quad and halls looking for litter. Take your time. Keep an eye out for any suspicious looking pieces of paper. Oh, by the way, how do you feel about underwear?"

"Boxers, definitely. Briefs just feel too restrictive."

"No, I mean girl's underwear. Specifically thongs. Have you heard of these... thongs?"

"Thongs? Eh. I prefer booty shorts myself. And sweatpants. Much less gross in my opinion. Less wedgification."

"So there's no epidemic beginning around here, in your opinion?"

"Thong epidemic? You'd need to ask someone else. I'm not really looking. But no. Definitely not."

"Thank you Mr. Park. Excused."

I practically kick in the door to Casey's classroom. I feel thirty pairs of eyes on my back as I walk up to the substitute. I recognize her now. "Hello Miss Kapsem. May I have a word with you outside regarding Casey?"

Miss Kapsem nods and says "Of course!" She looks prepared. I bet she's done this before.

Silence permeates the halls. Breathing it in, I temporarily forget what I'm doing out here. I just want to be present here, now, without obsessing about future problems or the consequences of past mistakes.

After giving me a minute to harangue her, Miss Kapsem decides to speak up. "The decision was unanimous, Mr. Kent. He was causing problems for everyone. The class was reluctant to do the usual lesson, of course, when they saw I was teaching. But everyone quieted down very quickly. Except for Casey. I told him to be quiet. Those around him even told him to shut up- their words, not mine. Then he'd be silent, but throw things, touch people, what have you. I didn't feel that it was my decision to kick him out, so I put it to a vote. It was unanimous. After he left the whole class applauded."

This doesn't sound like the respectful, informative boy I just talked to. I can see now that as soon as Casey saw the substitute at the front of the class he knew that he could get kicked out of the class easily and wouldn't miss anything important or pay any penalties. Miss Kapsem's tactics need to be addressed, however. "I appreciate how you took back the attention of your class and maintained authority and control. Good job. But do you see why you can't vote someone out? Just kick them out. You have that power."

"I guess I just wanted Casey to understand that it wasn't me who couldn't stand him. It was every other student in the class. I wanted him to see that he had no friends, no backup. Did you talk to him? Did he seem troubled?"

I think back. "No. Not at all actually. He seemed very insouciant, actually. That's why you need to just send them to my office immediately. With all due respect, you're a sub. Just appreciate an attentive class while you have one."

A sigh escapes her lips. "Yes, sir."

I giver her a half-hug. "Call me Adam, please. One day, you'll be throwing subs to the sharks while you take the day off to drink tea and read romance novels. Believe me." As I hear the door to the classroom click shut, my stomach audibly gurgles. I can't remember the last time I ate. I though it was just an hour ago, but perhaps not. Time to check on Mr. Caplan's home ec class, perhaps sample some marble cake or gingerbread houses.

Unfortunately when I get there I find that the class is empty except for Scooter the janitor. I would leave except... what is Scooter doing? Did he just empty the trash and recycling into the *same container?* Sacrilege! I charge into the room, burning questions on my tongue. How long have you been doing this? Do you have any respect for the system, any respect for the environment? Has this school actually recycled anything in the past eight years at all?

Hearing me enter, Scooter gives me a blank look. Blanker than usual, it seems. Suddenly I remember that this is the man who found Raymond's body. This is the man who could have seen me enter and leave Raymond's class the afternoon before. My rage evaporates like rain on hot asphalt.

"Hello Scooter."

"Hello Principal." He places the recycling bin back next to the trash receptacle. Is he mocking me?

"So, sorry to bring up such an emotional subject so soon, but what exactly did you tell the Detective about Raymond?"

"Same thing I told you. Showed up at five thirty and he was just lying there, dead as a doornail. Called you. Didn't touch anything."

"So you didn't see anything? Didn't see anyone around?" Unreadable expression, inscrutable as any I've seen on anyone's face. "Is there anything you need to better handle the grief that you must be feeling? Anything at all?"

He shakes his head.

"Okay then," I say, quickly glancing at the commingled detritus in his cart. "Happy... uh...."

"Rosh Hashanah."

"Right."

I take a seat on the tennis bleachers. Normally, I'd be recalling all the day's accumulated issues right now, coming up with courses of action, plans of attack, and worst case scenario contingency plans. I'd have a solution to the Koont dramatics. I'd already know how to repair the damaged recycling system. I'd know how to take revenge on Lincoln High for the death of my mascot. And yet, all I feel is an emptiness of mind. Bayview, for all its flaws, is still mine.

Monica Bastida, junior, walks by and does a double take. "Principal Kent? Shouldn't you be at the rally right now? For the big game?"

Oh yeah, the big game! Maybe that's why I'm so relaxed. Everything pales in comparison to the game. "You're very right. Let's walk to the multi purpose room together, shall we?"

The band's interpretation of "Smoke on the Water" finishes up. Then the seniors compete in one-legged relay races against the juniors. Jordan Starks plays the star spangled banner on electric guitar and picks the final notes with his teeth. I don't need to make a speech. I don't even need to go up there. But I guess I do; face time and all that.

At the podium, I sweep my gaze across the bleachers. Good turnout. "Alrighty," I say, "Let's give Lincoln High a run for their money! You can show your support by purchasing anything your budget allows from the student store. Every little bit helps, even pencil erasers or those little pins with the amusing cartoons. Thank you all, I am always impressed by your display of school spirit." I give a small wave.

"That's it?"

I can't tell who said that. While arching for the culprit I am taken aback by the sea of expectant and disappointed faces before me. "Er, yes. Let loose the dogs of war and all that. Don't get into any altercations with the Lincoln High students please! Let's shame them with our civility!" I give the small wave again.

"Where's our mascot?" A different voice this time, followed by a low rumble of voices.

"Oh, it got a little vandalized by someone. It might not even have been Lincoln High. It just needs a little cleaning. Don't worry about it."

"Fuck Lincoln High!" yells Casey Park.

"Now that's uncalled for. Remember, civility and good sportsmanship. Winning isn't everything.

"Fuck Lincoln High!" yells Casey Park.

"Fuck Lincoln High!" the row choruses.

"Fuck Lincoln High!" The cry is taken up quickly by what sounds like the entire stadium. Pure blood lust now. Rage. A thirst for not just victory but the shaming of their enemies.

"I love you all," I say into the microphone, and I have to exit quickly so they don't see my eyes tear up. For their sake, I hope they see some blood spilled tonight.

Halftime and the score is tied. The stands are packed tighter than I've ever seen theme. The noise is constant and deafening. I'm to the side of the stands in a secluded spot insulated from the noise and commotion. I care about this game, I really do, but for

67

some reason I just want to hide from sight and listen to the crowd. I can't even see the scoreboard from here.

"Hi," says a musical voice. It's the girl with the green eyes.

The din quiets to a murmur. The game is totally unimportant in the big scheme of things.

"Hello! I pride myself in knowing the names of all my students, but for some reason yours escapes me."

"It's Sera." The way she pronounces it is miles away from plain old boring "Sarah".

"Sera? As in '*que sera sera*'? Is that Celtic? Mayan? Krio? What kind of name is that?"

"I'll tell you that if you tell me how old you are."

She's the last person I would ever tell. Why? I break eye contact before it becomes unprofessional. Just another student. Just another student. I repeat the mantra as I pretend to watch the big game.

"Have you heard the phrase lick it or click it?"

Were her eyes really green? Maybe they were hazel. I need to sneak another look just to be sure.

"No.Why?" I ask. "What does it mean?"

She must not have heard me. She's obviously engrossed by the game. Just making small talk, like me.

"Can I see your driver's license?" I ask. Where did that come from?

"Why, so you know what color my eyes are?" she smiles.

"Do you even have a driver's license?"

"Yay Steve!" she screams. Oh yeah, Steve.

"Is it still tied? I can't see the score."

I can't read her expression. "Do you even care about the game? What's the matter with you? What did you do with our Principal?" Now I'm the one without an answer.

I actually pay attention to the game now. We score a field goal. Then Lincoln High does. It's utter pandemonium. I start to feel that old feeling. The electricity in the air. The smell of grass and fried food. The bright lights. We must win this game. Victory tonight will heal Bayview's emotional cuts, and defeat will permanently kill its spirit. This I know for certain.

A cheer rises through the air. A Lincoln High player lies on the ground, immobile. On closer inspection I see that his shin is bent in the middle. Like sharks, once my students see the enemy's blood, they only hunger for more.

"Wow. That's pretty gnarly."

"Yes," I agree.

Our possession. Their possession. They line up for another field goal. "No. No! NO!" The emotion in Sera's voice is breathtaking. I want to tell her it's just a game but I can't say it because I'm the Principal. I watch the football sail perfectly between the goalposts and the sudden silence in the stadium rips my heart into strips.

Three minutes left. My players advance up the field like a single entity, like a machine made of human components.

There's forty seconds left and twenty yards to victory when Steve Ortiz sprains his ankle. He gives the crowd a genuine smile as he limps to the bench.

"It over," I say.

"It's not over," Sera yells angrily, directly to me.

For the life of me I can't remember the second string quarterback's name.

"Now taking the field... number thirty one... BRANDON NELSON!"

Not him. Oh God. Not the bane of my existence personified. He's going to throw the game away just to make me suffer. He'll relish it like nothing else. I can't look. I turn my back to the field and look at the stars.

"He's got the ball! You have to watch!"

68

I just stare at the stars. They don't care about any of this. I can't watch my school die at the hands of a student I couldn't fix.

"Nelson throws to Michaelson!"

My students take a breath as one and hold it.

"I'll *make* you watch." Sera's small hands grip my head and twist like she's trying to snap my neck.

Touchdown.

"We did it, Sera!" I turn to her and yell, but she's already vaporized into thin air. She was probably never even here in the first place. Just my imagination.

There's nothing more to say. I know true inner peace. A single pelvic thrust in Chu's direction that I know she sees and then I go sit in a dark corner of the stadium and watch the celebration and walk of shame until the lights go out and I'm the last one left and then I sleep under the stars and finally don't dream.

11.

When I wake up my first thought is, "Did that really happen? Did we really win?"

My second thought is, "I need a hit so bad right now."

Everything itches. I bite my nails so my scratching doesn't scar my forearms. I am not looking forward to this day. I hate my employees. I hate this city. I hate this whole bankrupt state. I hate the Gazette. A lot. I hate that I can't punish it's author. I hate that I'm losing control of my school. I hate Detective Cooper and Scooter and Koont. I hate hate hate Brandon Nelson, even though he won us the game. I hate litter. I hate Tyler and Jesse and Jesse's father. I hate Chu and Lincoln High and I hate that I'm not happy about winning the game. I hate myself and my weaknesses. I hate the clouds and I hate the sky and the birds. I hate this *itching*. I hate everything about everything. Except the school.

Deep breaths. You can do this. It was just one momentary lapse. Not a relapse. Focus on getting this school back under your control.

It takes an eternity to get to my office. It takes five seconds after I sit down for Chris to walk in.

"Hello, Adam."

"Chris."

"I'd like to talk to you about the pelvic thrusting."

"What pelvic thrusting?"

"At the game last night. I was checking the video and I noticed your pelvic thrusting."

"It was one lightning quick pelvic thrust. Singular. A single thrust."

"Okay. It seems a little unprofessional though. I don't think anyone saw it-"

"No one except Chu. She saw it. She felt it in her soul. If she has one."

"It is a little unprofessional. I'd just like you to be aware of that, and ask you to try not to do it again."

I can handle this behavior from pretty much anyone except Chris. "You know what's unprofessional, in my opinion?" I start ticking them off on my fingers. "Leaving me alone to be ambushed by my faculty. Failing to fix the budget. Accusing your boss of not adequately doing the job he's been at for longer than you've even been here. And then telling your boss what to do!" I'm having trouble catching my breath. It's like I have asthma or something.

"Fine, fine," he smiles. Why can't I bask in the afterglow of last night's victory like he is? "Don't have a cow, man."

"I don't have a cow. What are you referring to? Are you saying I would be better as a farmer?"

"What? No, it's a Simpsons joke. You must have heard of the Simpsons!"

"The television? I don't watch the new shows."

My VP's brow furrows. "It's been on for like 25 years. How old are you?"

I don't answer that. "That is an extremely unprofessional question. Please get out of my office and go do something besides questioning my mental acuity. I need to make sure the budget is balanced by the end of the week, which you seem unable to do."

He's still smiling. "Sure thing, Adam. I hope you haven't already forgotten about the big game. That was amazing." He's actually whistling as he walks away. I try not to begrudge him his cheerfulness.

I can't wait until the budget is balanced. After that, I need to make sure this school is prepared for all of mother nature's many disasters. And I also need to create a plan in case of a schoolwide lockdown. Most of all, this pathetic teacher-instigated rebellion needs to be squashed. A familiar feeling creeps into my intestines and intensifies my uneasiness regarding rebellion. Oh no. Not now.

School hasn't even started yet but apparently that doesn't prevent the distribution of the Gazette. And by distributed, I mean stacked in a neat pile outside the front doors. NOW AVAILABLE IN THE STUDENT STORE: YOUR OWN ASSES.

Now that's not very fair. I carry the entire stack to the dumpster and throw it in. Then I climb inside and mix it in with the wet garbage and then stomp it to the bottom. Take that, whoever you are! I will bury you like the malignant tumor you are.

I walk back to my office to attempt some silent meditation. I'm stopped by Ginny the office lady, who says, "Roger Folson is here to see you, Adam."

Who? I follow her gesture and see the security camera man. Ah yes, the security cameras. I should peruse their constant stream of candid information more often. "Roger! My man! Please come into my office. Welcome back!" Once we're inside and both comfortably seated, I ask, "What can I do for you?"

He places a clipboard with a piece of paper clipped to it. I see a dotted line waiting for my signature. "I'm here to do the annual camera maintenance."

Excellent! Here's a consummate professional of the highest order. Chris could learn from Roger. "Will this cost the school anything?"

"It says on there," he explains and points a figure on the paper. It is not small.

"But that's almost as much as I paid for the installation!"

"Yes, sir. I'm doing the exact same thing: cleaning each camera inside and out, checking all the wiring and lenses, bringing any lost feeds back up, etc. It'll probably take two days."

He conveniently forgot to mention this when he installed the system. "I apologize, Roger, but the school cannot afford this right now. As a matter of fact, we're actually trying to avoid bankruptcy. I'm afraid there's no wiggle room."

He doesn't appear shocked or puzzled. It seems like this isn't new to him. "I see. That's a shame. The cameras should be good for another year or so. After that, I don't know if I'll be able to restore the system without a full physical overhaul. That's extra."

"Of course. Thank you for coming. I appreciate your candor."

He slides the chair back and stands. "I'm not sure what to tell my boss, though. This is the first time something like this has happened."

I'm sure. "You can tell your boss that I've been here long enough to know extortion when I see it." He tips his hat and exits without another word. Annual maintenance. Right. I should check out the monitor room, just to be sure.

Of course the monitor room is functioning perfectly. A wall of screens provide a constant barrage of footage that's all recorded straight to the many hard drives. Maybe one screen is a little choppy. I'll have the programming class make fixing it part of the midterm. No sweat. I should do my drugs in here from now on. Not that I'll do that ever again. This room is my panopticon.

Not that this is a prison. In prison there are things such as the Hole, also known as "segregation" or "solitary confinement". In the Hole you're alone for twenty three hours a day. You have one hour a day for recreations which is spent alone in what could be compared to a dog cage. This is not a prison. In Bayview I kick you out as punishment. In prison they keep you *in*.

I mean "panopticon" in the sense that everyone is in a state of conscious visibility. They can see the cameras. They can see each other. But they can't see the person behind the camera. It's enough to know that I'm here. It makes everyone safe.

I need to urinate and get the poison out of my system. At the urinal I peruse a small amount of graffiti on the walls: small text written in felt pen. It's vandalism, but it's also an outlet for creative expression and an opportunity to see the inner thoughts of my students. And cleaning it up gives Scooter something to do.

God bless our troops! Reads one. Underneath someone has written: *especially our snipers.* Another reads: *here I sit/ straining and stretchin,/ trying to pop out/ another Texan.* I've never been to Texas. Maybe they are all pieces of excrement. I spend the next few racking my brain about the budget and the Gazette while walking from bathroom to bathroom examining any graffiti I can find. Who profits by publishing such demonic slander? Who profits? There's not very much writing on the walls, but I'll still make a note of it in tomorrow's bulletin. *The water fountains taste like blood.* Next to this: *don't eat your mom out on her period.* I approve.

Now I slowly patrol the halls, scratching. Trisha Chamberlain passes by, waves, and half a second later I do a double take. "Trisha? Can I speak to you for a minute?"

"Sure!" Her lips practically drip with a purple, glistening, smelly ooze.

"That seems like an... unbecoming amount of lip gloss."

She immediately takes offense. "What do you know? You're an old man! It's not against the dress code!"

"You're completely right. And please don't feel like I'm passing judgement, and I feel that a bit of lip gloss is okay. But the widely accepted convention is that lip gloss should accentuate the natural color of the lips, not cover them up in layers of possibly toxic sludge. And I can smell it from here"

She purses her lips while she thinks of her next remark, and when they part strings of gunk still connect them. "Well, I could be wearing lipstick!"

"Now that actually *is* against the dress code. Do you know what lipstick's for? It's for classy parties, so if a woman was kissing some guy's mouth or... his mouth, it get smudged and everyone can see it. Keep it classy, alright? And I know it tastes good. That's not the point. Good talk." I need to keep moving. I feel a bit manic, a bit too talkative. I flex my hands so I don't scratch myself so much.

A shriek punctures my eardrums. My head whips back and forth and I crouch in a defensive posture. "What was that? What in God's name *was* that!"

"... the lunch bell?" The speaker is Monica Bastida. There's only amusement in her voice; no judgment.

"I know that. Yes. Actually, I wanted to talk to you, Monica," I try to come up with something to say. "Shouldn't you be going to lunch? You're going the wrong direction."

"I know! I'm not hungry.".

"Monica? Come on."

Sighing, she mutters, "I'm going to the hallway inside B−wing. The one behind the classrooms? It's empty at lunch."

"Why?"

"I'm helping some people with their homework. Actually," she straightens up, "I'm tutoring some people. The Spanish classes here kinda help white kids learn Spanish, but there's no class to teach English to the... non-white kids."

I am surprised. I shouldn't be. Yelena is a perfect example of what I want my students to be. "That's great! I'll tell you what, you can do this during lunch, after school, and even before school if you want- though that seems unfairly taxing on you. In return, you are excused from any language classes you are taking, and I will make sure you receive an A in them. Who's your Spanish teacher?"

"I'm actually taking German."

"Who's your German teacher then?"

"Mr. Hotz."

"If Mr. Hotz complains, I will berate him. You can watch. You are doing a good thing Yelena. I'm proud of you."

"Thanks Mr. Kent!" She skips away. That was good. That was unquestionably a positive thing I just did. I do that sort of thing all the time. I am the Principal. It's what I do. Unlike the Superintendent. Speaking of which, I need to check in with him. Make him feel good about himself.

When I get there it becomes clear that he's medicated himself for the day. Vodka this time, I think, given the plastic bottle of tonic water, tray of squeezed limes, and flushed complexion. "Adammmm! Good to see you! Terrible, that whole business with Reginald Paba. Terrible. I hope everything is going alright in the aftermath?"

"Yes, I believe so. The parents are very sympathetic and understanding, the students are cheerful and no longer afraid, and the guilty parties are in jail where they belong."

"Excellent! Good work. *Hic* Is there anything else you might want to tell me about this whole murder business? Anything the police have found out? They won't tell me anything."

"I'm in the same situation you are. They're keeping me totally in the dark."

Superintendent Burnside stares at me. The rims of his eyes are even redder than his face. There's something in those red rims I haven't seen before. Not depression, not frustration, not even anger. Suspicion, perhaps. "They haven't told you anything? Nothing about whether Tyler and Jesse are still suspects?"

"They're still in jail."

"That's not what I mean." He scratches his head, unsure now of what he meant. The vodka seems to be doing the job for me. Whatever kick he was on, now he's just inebriated. "I'm just wondering. That's really all I do in here. Maybe a meeting every now and then. Don't they want me?"

I'm not sure who "they" are so I stay silent.

"I mean, I'm here! You know? I'm capable. I'm not sure exactly what my job entails anymore, but I'm sure it will come back to me. If you see Jackson or Burke," probably his superiors, "Give them some hints that I'm... willing to work. They might think they're giving me what I want. This cushy job, the fat paycheck, whatever. But this isn't what I want."

"I've never met them, sir. You're my only boss." That seems to cheer him up a little.

"Alright then. Please if you need anything, if you want to relax, have a sip of something, come on by. I'm... always... here."

"Thank you, George. I will certainly do that."

Ginny the office Lady waves to me as I head to the monitor room. "Brandon Nelson came in a few minutes ago. He said that it's on. Do you know what that means? He left before I could ask him."

I do know what it means. And I hope I am strong enough see it through.

I leave Bayview early so I can conceal myself behind a stand of trees with a clear view of the bus stop. Eventually, the bus offloads four kids. I recognize Brandon immediately and three other students. And Wes is already there.

When did he show up?

He looks just as I remember him, except for the stubble, noticeably paler skin and scar under his right eye. He waves to my students, tries to initiate conversation. They wave back, but keep walking. Good for them. I trained them well in avoiding human scum. He looks very puzzled when Brandon also passes him by. Wes tries to stop him but then thinks better of it. I cease digging my nails into my palm. If I saw him touch any of my students I'd rip his arms off. It's time.

"Wes! My former student! Well met, friend!" Wes's eyes bulge when he sees me, but then hardens his gaze and hunches over, putting his hoodie up. I guess he's not new at this drug dealer stuff.

"Mister Kent! Whatchu need, whatchu need?"

He knows I know exactly what he's up to. He doesn't know about me and Brandon but I'm positive he knows I've been watching him. "I'm sorry? Wes, I just want to talk about what you've been up to. Maybe why you're here trying to talk to my current students."

"Yo, Adam, time is money. Whatchu need dawg?"

First name basis, I see. I'm not itching anymore or even grinding my teeth. My body knows what my mind does not. Deep down, it's time to admit that my decision was made for me that night in the handicapped stall.

"How much for an eight ball?"

He quotes a price.

"That's reasonable," I reply, because it is.

"You get the Principal hook up this time. Next time you get the regular customer discount, know what I'm sayin?"

"Half of it now. When I know the quality, I'll pay you in full for the other half."

"Yo, I don't step on shit! This is the raw!"

"This isn't the raw, don't treat me like an idiot."

"I don't usually front the product, but I know you're trustworthy and whatnot. You run a tight ship." We close the deal with several handshake-like maneuvers.

"From now on, you only do business with Brandon or myself. I find any other student with your product, and I step on your face. Repeatedly. You are no longer my student, understand? I have no qualms about burying you under the dirt next to my other problems."

Wes doesn't blink. "Sounds good. That cuts into my profits, but I'm cool with it." The terms have been agreed upon so I guess there's nothing left to say. I walk away without saying another word.

I know how this goes. He's just a drug dealer now. I don't feel ashamed in the least. The more I think about it, I'm really protecting my students from him in the most mutually beneficial way possible.

I don't know where I'm walking. I cross Oakmont to the west side of town, hop down to the train tracks. Eventually the graffiti shows up. The track curves, and I climb back up to 16th avenue. The brown walls and tinted glass in front of me indicate that I'm in front of Central High, and I stroll through at a leisurely pace. Cracked glass, busted air conditioning units, non-functioning water fountains. Overcrowded. Underfunded.

"There was a stabbing downtown not two months ago. I buy hard drugs miles away, in front of my own school. So why is *this* the bad part of town? Because brown people live here?" I don't know why I ask this out loud. There's no one to hear me.

12.

The room is pure orange from the tile to the ceiling. It's packed with people

73

standing and sitting on the chairs and the floor. No receptionist. Muzak piped in from hidden speakers. Two stainless steel elevator doors reflect the harsh fluorescents recessed somewhere above.

"This is obviously a waiting room. What's everyone waiting for? Isn't anyone going to take the elevator?"

A man in priest's garb walks up to me, hand in hand with an Arab wearing a red and white-checked turban. "This is purgatory, son. Once you get too bored, just take the elevator to the afterlife you deserve."

Makes sense to me. "I'm going to do that right now. Why is everyone else just waiting in purgatory?"

The Arab draws his scimitar and starts waving it around, boredom draping his features. I realize that he and the priest are stuck in here as well. "I don't know why they're here," replies the priest, "but I can tell you why I'm still here. It's reverse psychology. You know reverse psychology?"

"Yes. I've sat in on plenty of introductory psych classes. I find them informative and very compelling."

"Of course. Well, the logic of the Good Book dictates that heaven is above us, and the fiery pits of hell below. But what if this is God's final test? What if the lake of fire resides above and below, and the truly penitent wait here until the end of days?"

Poor bastard. "The lake of fire seems preferable to waiting here forever. At least in hell I'll have interesting company."

I shoulder through the mob and press the down arrow. The button lights up. One minute passes. Five. The elevator isn't coming. Someone taps my shoulder. It's Tyler! He looks very ill. His eyes are pure white. "Tyler! Can you help me?"

His cheeks balloon and he vomits blood all over me. Clots of viscous red liquid bounce off my cheeks. He starts clawing at my eyes. I scream. Tyler's rictus is red, red, red.

I jerk up from my desk. The side of my face is wet. Touching it and looking at my fingers I figure out that it's just drool. Wow, that was one hell of a daydream! That's all it was, though. I can tell the difference between daydreams and waking stimulant-induced hallucinations. Once I start hallucinating I know it's time for a tolerance break. I mean it's time to stop for good.

My crumpled suit indicates that I wore these clothes yesterday and slept in my office. Unlike Detective Cooper, I have self respect and more than one suit. After I change into my gray flannel suit and periwinkle tie I consider my plans for the day. Huh. I guess I have no plans. That's suits me just fine. I excel at improvisation.

The metal handrail on the eastern stairs is abraded. Someone recently rode a skateboard on this rail, griptape down. Impressive as the darkslide may have been, it is totally against the rules and the possibility of future darkslides must be terminated. I now recall a recently confiscated skateboarding magazine's two-page glossy spread of a professional skateboarder photographed grinding down this rail. It is indeed long and beautiful, but it can't be fully appreciated with some miscreant with no job prospects scraping the shine off it. I make a note to tell Scooter to mount some small metal brackets at intervals down its length. I should also print a reminder in the bulletin that skateboarding is illegal on campus, even after hours. Maybe put something in there about helmet laws too. My throat's sore for some reason.

I smell something delicious. I catch Cody Lee at a distance, holding a steaming cookie. He doesn't look worried when he sees me.

"Cookies are not on sale yet! In fact, they are just now being baked. Did you steal that fresh baked cookie, Cody?"

"No. I mean, I took it, but come on. There were like two hundred of them in there! Plus they cost like fifty cents for three of them."

"Are you aware that Bayview is undergoing a budget crisis at the moment? Of course you don't. If you were, you would know that each cookie is the difference between a budget surplus and unending debt. You are threatening the school's very future. How often have you done this?"

"Just once! Really!" When someone follows up a statement with 'really', the statement is usually false.

"Adam! Adam!" James Hetfield the chemistry teacher tugs at my sleeve like a petulant child. I ignore him.

"Eat it. Now."

"But it's too hot!"

"That's your own fault. Eat it now or I suspend you for theft." He takes a tentative bite. "Shove it in there! You have thirty seconds!"

Munch munch. "Ow! Ow!" I scrutinize him as he swallows. "That actually hurt, Mr. Kent!"

"Adam!"

"One second, please. You must realize, my young student, that that didn't hurt as much as theft of fresh baked cookies hurts this school. Tell this cautionary tale to your friends. And buy lots of cookies." Now I give Mr. Gutierrez my attention. "What is it?"

"Someone put glue in my locks!"

I go cold all over. "Someone has vandalized your classroom door?"

"No, no! My car doors! Someone squirted glue in them, and the trunk too! I can't get in!"

"Oh, okay. That's not school property. I hope you don't expect the school to pay for a tow truck."

His mouth opens and closes like a trouts'. "That's not fair!"

I don't have time for this. I'm sure this man is plotting my usurpation every night before he sleeps. "Do you enjoy having a job in this double dip recession? Yes? Then it is in your best interest that this school doesn't spend money on frivolous things like tow trucks."

He can't argue with my logic bomb so he just walks away as if recovering from a spanking. The nerve of that man! What's next? Oh yes, one of my substitute teachers has requested a meeting. I greet the office ladies warmly as they speak to parents in extremely uncaring tones. I make sure to wipe residue off the desk before I call in the sub.

"Hello, sir. I'm Richard Vance. I've been subbing here for two years tomorrow. Thank you for taking the time to see me again."

"Great to see you! Students haven't been giving you too much trouble?"

"Nope. I've enjoyed all my time here." I already know this. There are really only two types of substitutes at this school: the terrified rookies who get torn apart by the students on a daily basis (they can smell weakness) and leave no longer interested in the field of teaching, and the hardened veterans who learn quickly and earn the students' respect with just the look in their eyes. Yusuf is in the latter category.

"I'm pleased to hear that. How can I help you?"

A prolonged breath. "I'd just like to say first off that I know you're a busy man. I'm not trying to rush you or anything. But... I'm curious how much progress you've made on my letter of recommendation. One from you would look very, very good on my application to graduate school."

So Yusuf is planning on leaving? Understandable, but I would loathe seeing such a valuable resource leave Bayview at such a time. "Certainly Richard. I'm sorry I haven't done that yet. I'd just like to say something first, and please take it with a grain of salt. But there are more people going to grad school than ever. More students, more schools, more bachelor's degrees. There are many Ph.D.'s in the job pool now. They are a dime a dozen, to be honest. Many of them work as unpaid or underpaid lab assistants and TAs for a decade, their doctorate dangling in front of their face like a burro's carrot. Their term for it is 'post grad hell'."

The only response I get is a wry grin. "Thanks for the info, Adam. But I am already aware of the situation. I'm planning on getting my masters.The programs are cheaper and more specialized. There's a program I'm looking at that's only two years. Grueling, but quick. And I'll make more money, it looks better than a bachelor's, and I avoid the postgrad hell facing most of the wannabe doctors."

Smart. I shouldn't have expected less from Yusuf. "I'll have it for you on Friday. Thank you for your years of service."

"Great! I appreciate the experience you've granted me. It was definitely an eye-opener. Here's something I typed up last night, just in case you're very, very busy and don't have the time to talk to others about my accomplishments. It's the cliffs notes of my time here I guess. I know your time is valuable and in short supply, unlike Ph.D.'s." We share a laugh. I'll be sad to see him go.

Once I'm alone again, I place Richard's notes it on top of my In/Out tray. Hmmm. I take a second look at it. The bottom tray is empty. The stack of paperwork on top is a precarious tower perhaps a foot tall. Maybe two feet. It defies gravity, actually wider on the top than the bottom. I blow off the dust, choking slightly on the ensuing cloud. Curious, I reach to the bottom, pull and out a random page. Yusuf's paper is lost in the avalanche that cascades to the floor. I examine what is apparently the minutes of a staff meeting, dated eighteen month ago. On the back neat handwriting reads, *If you actually read this I need to talk to you about some budget issues. –Chris.* I feel validated in the way I deal with paperwork. The budget was brought to my attention eventually. I didn't need to read this paper at all! I'm wasting my time looking at it right now, in fact.

That shrieking noise again! Oh, it's just the lunch bell. Right. Is it lunch already? I scratch an itch and feel immediately satisfied.

In the cafeteria, I hobnob with my students as I eat. Two helpings of delicious food and I still feel famished. Two more helpings and I feel satiated enough to sit at the table contentedly and let the conversations about relationships, homework, wakeboarding, online videos and so much more wash over me like a warm tide.

Afterward I check on the student council meeting and help them decide on a theme for the prom. Everyone is still gleefully chattering about Lincoln High's shamefaced defeat. It feels good to siphon away Chu's sloppily cultivated school spirit for my own purposes. To make them feel even better, I gift the council with the authority to decorate the windows at the entrance to the school. I feel so good that for an instant I forget about the... oh no. No no no.

I can sense it nearby. Where? The hallways are empty and immaculate, but I don't feel satisfied in the least. I survey the quad: no litter in sight. I hate to say it, but it's too clean. I'm armpit-deep in the trash can before I pull it out. A soggy issue of the Gazette, dated today. PRINCIPAL KENT'S ALL-FAT DIET SHOWS RESUTS. I should have known that when there's nothing about the institution to complain about that the writer would resort to cheap personal attacks. I'm not fat at all! So what if my belt is one hole wider than it was last month? So what if the shoulders of my blazer feel tight? This simply betrays the Gazette's own lack of original journalism. If you can call it journalism and not hate speech.

I try to sit in on the introductory psych class, but it's no use. I can't concentrate on anything and my internal monologue drowns out the teacher's lecture. I consider trying to write some more of <u>The Principal's Guide to Success </u>but I know deep down that the words won't come. A retreat to my office is the only solution.

Doing a line off the glassy surface of my beautiful mahogany desk helps a bit. I'll show them. I'll become more fit than they could ever believe! I have excess energy to burn, and an office to myself. "Hold my calls!" I yell.

I start out with fists-to-the-ground pushups, followed by elbows to the ground pushups, back arched. Then in the same position I move my legs back and forth like I'm sprinting, one after the other. Then both legs at the same time. Then both legs sweeping in circles like I'm swimming. I'm pouring sweat now so I take my jacket off. Now I'm on my back with my shoes wedged under the desk. I sit up, grab the desk and follow through to a standing position, then back down. I repeat the movement until I can't breathe. Then I get the pillow in my closet, lie back under the desk, arch my back with my head pressing against the pillow, and move my stomach up and down. Then I turn over and put my weight on my head with my back arched and my hands clasped behind my back. My chest burns. And my shoulders and my waist. I hurt all over. I go back to pushup position and lift up my left arm and right shoulder, and then the reverse. I try to go back to pushup position again and just straighten out with my weight on my elbows but I collapse. All I can do is lie on the floor and appreciate every scorching breath.

It's actually quite easy to get a full workout, even when you're confined to a single room. That's why convicts have such impressive musculature.

Endorphins coursing in my bloodstream, a fresh application of deodorant and a change of clothes later and I'm ready to finish the day at a strong, brisk pace.

But now I am almost out of stuff. And I don't have time to walk to the downtown café and meet Wes at the designated time. And I won't bring myself to speak to Brandon, who is no doubt gone already. My throat is excruciatingly sore, probably because of the smoke I'm inhaling.

Smoke?

I may be the one wearing clean clothes, but I feel as dirty as Detective Cooper looks. Same coat, different tie. Before he can speak I snatch the cigarette from his lips and dispose of it with relish. He must have been expecting that because he doesn't even react, just launches into whatever speech he has planned.

"Trial's coming up, buddy, and fucking *soon*. You ready to earn your keep?"

The trial. "When exactly will that be, Detective?"

"I got a question, Adam. Just out of curiosity," he changes the subject so quickly he must not know, "how many girls are diagnosed with ADD?"

"I don't know. You should ask a psychiatrist."

"I ain't asking my psychiatrist anything, that pole smoker. Funny, though, innit? Parents don't like their boy's behavior? They put him on Concerta or some other pill. Fucking legalized speed. Don't like what their son says? He's 'bipolar'. That's a new one, huh? Put him on Zyprexa, zombify that poor fucker. Or other pills with side effects you wouldn't believe. Girls just get away with it. Why? Boy gets asthma-"

"Wait, I'm fairly confident that asthma's a legitimate medical condition."

"Bullshit. I had asthma as a kid, or so they said. Look at me. My lungs are fine. No breathing problems here."

I need this man out of my life. Time to ask a personal question. "What kind of pills are you on?"

"Meth pills," he says, followed by that cackling cough-laugh I'm too familiar with. "Funny though, the way the world works. You smell something? You're sniffing a lot."

Thought I wasn't doing that. "Am I? I guess it's just the second hand smoke I smell as it gives me cancer."

"Absolutely no proof of that. Read some science journals, professor."

"You read science journals?"

"Hell no! I don't have time to sit on my ass all day and be an academic. I do murders. I'll only remind you of this one more time: without your testimony, I have to reinstate the DNA evidence. And those unidentified epithelials, they'll speak for you. Are we clear, Principal?" He pops the p in 'principal' and spittle lands on his chin, which he wipes off with his emerald tie.

"Very clear. Is there anything new you'd like to tell me?"

He scratches his neck stubble. "Just keep your nose clean until the trial, if you know what I mean."

"Mine's much cleaner than yours, Detective." When he's gone, I go back to my office and do what I have to do.

13

Another monitor is going to static. The first one is completely dark. I still have plenty of screens to peruse and stare at though. More than enough. I don't know how long I've been in here staring at the live feeds and reviewing old footage for any hint of the Gazette writer doing his evil deeds. I guess I've been here all night. I've got that itchy feeling that signals that I need to do my exercises.

Wait! On the top row of monitors, a white face passes from one to another impossibly fast. It has black eyes like a demon. I rewind the feed. The face doesn't reappear. I rewind it again but there's nothing to see. I rub my eyes. That doesn't count as a hallucination since it was over so quickly. My exercises last longer than usual so I can purge any residual poison out of my system.

My students appear cheerful as usual. Not a single one of them even remembers that they used to have a horrible Spanish teacher or classmates named Tyler and Jesse. I wish I could know what each one is thinking. I can see on the cameras what they do when no one's looking but I can't quite tell what they think.

The sound of hard heels echo on the cement. Chu's heels. She greets me with a nod and a forced smile. Finally showing her face! Didn't think I'd see her until next semester. This will be satisfying. "Principal Chu? To what do I owe the exquisite pleasure of your presence here after your terrible loss on the field oh so long ago?"

"There's always next year. I'm here because Chris asked me for help with the school's financial difficulties."

I know Chris's behavior has been less subservient as of late, but this is on an entirely different level. I feel like a knife just slipped between my vertebrae. "I don't know what Chris has been telling you, but the last thing I need right now is a speech from a sellout like you!"

"I've heard it all before. From you, from the parents, from everybody. The fact remains that Lincoln High's financial situation is much more stable than the situation Chris has been telling me about."

"Chris is misinformed, then."

"Just hear me out. Please. Do you remember the advice I've been giving you since day one? Despite what you may think, I do know what I'm doing when it comes to running a high school.

"Now, it's all well and good to cut costs, but sometimes that does more harm than good. What you need to do is start constructing new additions to the school! Retrofit, upgrade, make the whole thing more 'earthquake safe'. Then, you can get some help from my friends at the credit union downtown. I've already vouched for your credit worthiness. Then," she lowers her voice to a whisper, "you can securitize the construction bonds into an over-the-counter derivative! The worst of the property loan crisis is over, despite what the talking heads on the news say. It's a global sovereign debt crisis now."

Most of the words she says don't make sense, but perhaps because of that nothing she says seems exactly wrong.

She sees I'm at least pretending to understand and continues, "It's completely legal. Every college there is reinvests their profits in mutual funds or certificates of deposit or other financial instruments. This way the school not only gets a facelift *and* a safer foundation, but you can reinvest the profits however you want!"

If a deal sounds too good to be true then it probably is. "I'm not a private school, Chu."

"Neither are the state's 'public' universities, but that doesn't stop them from raising fees exorbitantly every year to fill the hole left by the government's financial failures. There are some cracks showing on your tennis courts, Adam."

That's crossing the line. Hypothetical money mumbo jumbo is fine, but no one suggests that I'm not maintaining my grounds. No one.

"You should stop giving me financial advice and focus on using your excess blood money to support the homeless, most of whom are former students of yours," I chortle. Perhaps I've been insulting her too much every year since she appears to take satisfaction from the personal jabs. "What have you done recently to support the homeless?"

"I buy liquor from them."

"What? You're far older than 21."

Chu shrugs. "You do what you gotta do to feel young again. Am I right?"

"I am young!" My rival shrugs again, hands me her card, and leaves the way she came. Oddly, I wish she would give me the finger again. I need to talk to Chris about this.

He's in his office poring over esoteric administrative paperwork. "I hear you've been talking to that earthworm who calls herself a principal behind my back! I demand an explanation!" I shout, though I can't seem to summon up any genuine rage. I don't know why.

Chris can tell. He takes a moment to mark his spot and then looks up at me, "The school's still bleeding cash. Your strategy of increasing product at the student store has actually cost the school money since no one's buying the new merchandise. Even though I will admit the new swag is of excellent quality."

"But... you need to spend money to make money!"

His eyes light up. "So you actually talked to Chu instead of insulting her ancestors! Great! What do you think of what she had to say?"

"Rubbish! I will not cook the books. That is immoral and insulting to even suggest."

"It's not cooking the books if everyone does it. Even if it doesn't work, it buys us some years to come up with something new. We need short term solutions until we have long term ones."

I can only think of one thing to counter Chris's onslaught of double-talk. "I know standardized tests are coming up, and I also know that our funding is directly tied to how our students score. Each student at Bayview is brilliant. I for one won't underestimate our students' intelligence. How high do we have to score on the test to buy us some time, as you so eloquently put it?"

At this, Chris put his pencil in his mouth and chews it thoughtfully. "That's a good question! That's why you're the boss, I guess," he admits. One or two minutes later he finishes up his calculations. "We can balance the budget by the end of the year if we score in the... ninety-ninth percentile."

"So we just need to score ninety nine percent better? That's not too bad! We can double our scores easy!"

"Uh, no we can't. Not easily. And the ninety ninth percentile actually means we need to score better than ninety nine percent of the schools out there."

I have no head for numbers. "Are you saying that our school is not better than ninety nine percent of the schools out there? I disagree with your lack of patriotism."

"I'm saying that depending on every one of our students to suddenly ace the SATs is not a feasible option."

"Well *you* come up with something then!"

"What do you think I'm doing every day? Come on. You know I'm trying. You know I care about this school just as much as you do."

"If you do you have a strange way of showing it." There's nothing more to say. Fighting doesn't solve this issue. It doesn't even make me feel better like it usually does. My throat really hurts.

"This is hard to say, but I don't really have a choice. I think it's time you look at the possibility of cutting salaries. Even yours and mine."

"Go ahead and cut mine. It's not about my paycheck."

Chris nods, says, "It's not about mine either," and goes back to whatever it is he does in here.

What else can I do? I could institute school uniforms. It would look nice. I could make them a little more expensive than the wholesale price, and get the money Bayview needs directly from the parents without costing the students anything. But I would be taking money from the less wealthy parents too. And the students would hate me. And I couldn't handle Koont's gloating.

No more money business today. That kind of stuff tends to sort itself out anyway. To distract myself, I study which girls are wearing whose letterman jackets and add more strings to the network in the evidence room, which I admit I've been neglecting. I hear rumblings of an altercation in the quad and as usual I break it up before a single blow lands. Unsurprisingly the fight is about a girl, and I alter the string network accordingly.

Next to the network I have an enormous bulletin board displaying a collage of Gazette pages I've been working on since the first one came out. I've underlined passages in red pen both for grammar correction and for possible tells that belie the writer's (or writers') identity. Along the bottom a row of small photographs stare back at me: Chu, Brandon Nelson, Tyler and Jesse's parents, Koont, Lincoln High's quarterback and various other persons arranged like a police lineup. Staring at all this for a solution feels like striking my forehead against an anvil.

I try to spend the rest of the day studying the security camera feed but I leave after I see that blurred clown face again out of the corner of my eye. I can't write. I haven't been able to put together a single sentence for weeks. I decide to sit in on James Hetfield's chemistry class. I could stand to learn a little about the universe's underpinnings today.

Ever the professional, James only acknowledges me with a second of eye contact before continuing the lesson. It's about electron shells, and staring at the neatly labeled diagrams of perfectly round valences soothes me. The universe is based on rules set in stone. Everyone follows these rules whether they want to or not. Heather Stimson raises her hand but James ignores her. I raise an eyebrow; that seems rather unprofessional of James. She continues to raise her hand.

James clears his throat. "Yes, Heather, I am aware of the Bible's stance on the origin of electron shells. You will have your usual sixty seconds at the end of class to voice your opinion.

"You mean voice the *facts*," she pouts.

I came to this class to relax, but now I fear the entire class can hear my teeth grind together. The universe does not follow the rules of some mainstream mistranslation of some ancient hodgepodge of myths! "Separation of church and state!" I want to scream. "Goat herders living thousands of years ago do not know more about how the universe works than your Chemistry professor!" My mouth manages to stay clamped shut. Good. The last thing I need is a student claiming I impinged upon her freedom of religious expression. How is Heather even in this class? This is AP Chemistry! Is there nowhere I can go for a few periods of quiet contemplation to quiet my rage?

At the end of the school day the answer turns out to be no but I'm not sure if that's because of others or because of my brain.

Café Luna is tiny, dimly lit and full of quiet tables away from any prying eyes or government surveillance. My mind can't make itself up about how to feel about Wes. I mean, I hate him. But he was my student and he provides what I need to make it through the day. I mean feel better. At least he doesn't judge me like every one of my coworkers. And he doesn't make small talk about the past or anything. I get my coffee, and the payment and exchange finish before the liquid is cool enough to drink. I lean back in my chair with the manila envelope firmly in my jacket, and act like I plan to sit here and drink coffee for the rest of the day.

"Hit me up when you wanna re-up," Wes grunts before he leaves the café. I watch him through the window and the moment he turns the corner I dash out of the building after him. I can tail a suspect like you wish you could, Detective. Within two blocks Wes stops, waiting for someone. I duck inside a bookstore on the corner and watch him from inside concealed behind a wall of mystery novels.

A light skinned African American man in his twenties walks up to my former student wearing a light gray sweater emblazoned with the word "Harvard" in crimson felt. They do something with their hands and walk away in opposite directions. I'm positive that Wes just handed off the part of my meager salary I could be anonymously donating to the school to this stranger. He looks one tenth the gangster Wes does, if that. I know how to follow the money, Chu. Maybe if I extort Wes's boss I'll have enough cash to reinvest in the school and prevent any sort of closure once and for all.

"Hi Mr. Kent," says Sera. She's behind the science fiction shelf. She's peeking at me through a gap between hardcovers.

"Hi." Did she see what I was doing? Does she know I was watching someone? Can she tell I have an envelope packed with drugs wedged in my coat?

"I sorta locked myself out of my apartment and my parents don't get home for another couple hours. Could you possibly get me a snack or a sandwich here? I'll pay you back."

"You don't have to pay me back! I'd love to get you something to eat but I don't...." I don't have any money. I spent it all on narcotics, you see. "I actually lost my wallet. I guess we're both making mistakes today."

"I have change. I think I could get us a coffee, at least."

"No, don't do that! I have some food at home," I speak without thinking and then cover my mouth like I could keep the words from being said. I don't think I actually have any food at home. I haven't for a while since I can just eat for free at the school anytime I want. "I think. Maybe."

"*Maybe* you have food in the house?" she giggles. "Is it close?"

What's close? Are we close to each other right now, even though we're on different sides of the aisle? Are we too close? Definitely. "It's nearby, I guess. But I don't know if...." I trail off again. *I don't know if you should trust me.* And she's barely listening, already bored. Bored and hungry. "Okay. How will your parents know where you are?"

She points to her back pocket. "Cell phone. You really need one- I always see Mr. Hasty running around trying to find you." I can't really afford one. I spend all my money on drugs now, you see.

I don't think we say one word on the walk to my house. It's very awkward. The entire way I obsess silently about how and where I live. It's a nice enough neighborhood: large trees on both sides of the street with touching canopies, well maintained lawns, and quiet residents. It's a nice enough house, too. White fence, clean driveway (no car), peaked roof and wooden walls painted sky blue. But the interior! I've had no time to make it normal!

Too late, we're already inside.

The entryway is bare. The living room is empty of everything; no couches, TV, lamps or pictures. The dining room doesn't even have a table. We walk into the kitchen, which is empty of everything except the fridge, sink and oven. The only object that distracts the eye from the shocking white expanse of the bare walls is a Polaroid of the front of the school taped to the fridge. Where did I get the tape from? What kind of impression am I making on Sera? She must think I'm absolutely insane.

She seems more perplexed than anything as her eyes slide around the room with nothing to latch on to. "Did you just move in or something?"

Illogically, I don't want to lie to her. I decide not to pretend anymore, for some reason. If I can actually stop pretending to be something I'm not, which seems to be exactly what I've been doing for eight years.

"Nope, this is just how I live," I smile, and shrug.

"Hmm. Very Zen. I like it, it's easy on the eyes." She spins like a dancer and opens the fridge. "And inside the fridge you have... an empty water bottle; a head of lettuce, gray; and a box of crackers, which is empty as well."

"I eat out most of the time."

"I don't see any Chinese food cartons."

"I tend to eat everything. All the time."

Sera either exhales in disbelief or sighs to express her hunger pangs. "Well, this seemed like a good idea in the bookstore."

"I'm sorry. I haven't had guests in a long time and I guess I let the house get this way."

"I think it was always this way, Mister Kent. Let me guess, the freezer is empty too. Oh my God!"

"What?" I envision the worst possible thing lurking in there. Maybe black mold or perhaps a severed caribou head. Anything could be in there.

"Frozen M&Ms! I loooove frozen M&Ms!" Sera tosses one almost to the ceiling and catches it in her mouth. In between crunches she asks, "Do you have anywhere to sit?"

I don't have any chairs anymore. Something bad happened to them, I think. "The carpet in the living room is very plush." So we sit on the living room floor and I watch her eat the mystery bag of M&Ms. They must be M&Ms. No drugs I know of taste like milk chocolate. "Can I have one?"

"I guess. I'm the guest here, but whatever." They actually taste better frozen.

After a while we chat about inconsequential things. Interesting places to go in the city and what my neighbors are like. Eventually we somehow get on the subject of racism. "I'm not Mexican, but I get so angry when I hear people talk about them like one single group when they obviously know nothing about the country or the culture. Some people just treat them as a race of people or some army of criminals with bad intentions. It seems like someone just needs to say the word 'Mexican' a certain way and it just delivers all the poisonous stereotypes at once, like a rattlesnake or something."

I think back to a time six years ago when I found out that an English teacher, Mr. something-or-other, was making certain hateful remarks against certain ethnic groups. Or people from a certain country. Whatever Mexicans are. And that's something I absolutely will not tolerate. I have an unspoken zero tolerance policy against racism and punish offenders harshly but fairly. This guy is being covertly racist and discriminating grade-wise against these people, and I can't do anything about it that follows the written rule of law. So I start tailing him every day, memorizing his routine, and one Friday night when he leaves to see a movie like he does every week I rush to the store and buy a baseball bat and a ski mask and then I break into his house and start destroying everything destructible I can find. Eventually I run out of stuff to break into pieces so I just wait in the rubble until he comes back home. When he opens the front door I pull him inside and speak Spanish-sounding gibberish at him for a while. Then I gesture at the side of his cranium with the bat and leave. Needless to say he didn't come into work again. I think he actually left town that night. I made sure to leave his car intact.

And I want to tell Sera this to make her feel better or maybe just to get it off my chest, but I don't. I'm still being honest with her, very honest. I'm just choosing what information to reveal. It's nice to just sit here and eat frozen M&Ms and be honest. I truly feel like myself and not like I'm wearing this blank mask I put on to keep the people around me oblivious and safe. I could get used to being honest like this.

"Mr. Kent?" From her tone she seems to want to tell me something very personal.

"You can confide in me about anything, Sera. Absolutely everything."

She still looks around like she's scanning for eavesdropper. Then she leans close and whispers, "I don't think Tyler and Jesse did it."

Oh well. At least I was honest for a little while.

Her cell phone suddenly rings ear-burstingly loud. She answers it and waves goodbye before walking out the door. When I wave back the gesture feels hollow. At least I'm still honest. And at least there's still some partially frozen M&Ms left in my empty house.

14.

I feel like a cheap prostitute. I pick up the phone for the thirtieth time today and call another small business owning parent. I have my first lines memorized. "Hello, Mr./ Mrs. _____ . How would you like to support our football team and our school as a whole... *at the same time!*" I'm not prostituting the school as much as I'm prostituting myself, but at least if I succeed at this I can keep Bayview public and equally open to everyone. Very few things nowadays are truly free. Maybe love, but I'm not too sure about that.

"But football season's almost over!" some complain to get out of doing their duty as a local business owner and payer of extremely low taxes.

"There's still two games left in the season, and I'm actually calling you before anyone else so you can get in on the ground floor of this operation and have all summer to design the advertisement that will be visible all next year!"

Once I've called the last person I head over to the student council's meeting room. "Does anyone know how the school can save money?" I ask, without begging at all.

"We can switch to more efficient light bulbs and toilets!"

"That's a very good idea, but that saves money in the future, while costing lots of money now. We need to save money now." Chris says the school is now hemorrhaging money, which I do not understand. How could the state's financial situation be worsening at such a brisk pace?

The students can't come up with anything else. I leave them to debate about whether feeding mice to the pet snakes kept behind glass in Mrs. Cross's biology class is wrong. I don't educate them that it's eat or be eaten outside my school grounds.

A quick stop in Chris's office. "A thought came to me recently," I say. "Do we make or lose money if a student tests out of Bayview early or opts for independent study?"

My VP rubs his chin stubble. I've never seen him anything but cleanly shaven. "With rare exception, students can't do either until senior year. The potential costs cancel out the lost money their presence would earn Bayview, even if they were in school everyday. And given that they want to leave here early they probably wouldn't still be here. I wouldn't worry about it."

"One more question. If a student opts to test out, does that reflect poorly on the school? On me?"

"Not at all. If they passed the required tests they obviously learned a lot in their time here."

"Still, the school experience as a whole is more than one or two tests. Every day is a test of some kind."

"Don't I know it," he sympathizes.

Hard time catching my breath at the top of the stairs. Not only that but my gums hurt and I think my teeth are a lot flatter than they were a month ago. The arms under my sleeves are red, swollen, and lined with scratch marks. I hide all these problems well. Maintaining a spotless image is something I am very good at by now. The students and staff suspect nothing.

Time for a meeting with the Judases I used to trust to shut up and do their jobs. As soon as everyone sits down they start talking all at once and eventually they're yelling so as to be heard over everyone else who's yelling, which is everybody. Coughs rack my body so bad my shoulders heave raggedly. They fall silent, maybe out of concern.

"Computers cannot replace teachers," I begin, "but it's getting close. We're almost there. An authority figure just needs to be in the room and the kids will learn more just spending time on the internet than they ever would from you failures. A teacher in a box is all I need. Some assembly required, ha ha."

Eye contact is made with every single person in the room before I continue, "Kids are not capital. But you 'educators' might as well be. You are only efficient tools for developing my human beings. Students are *my* human beings. Until they leave they are my human beings. God help you if you try and hinder the growth of my human beings."

"Education is not the same as learning. You all used to know that. Now you are nothing but pedagogical reflex motions. Take your day one student at a time, for the love of God, and leave me out of it. Please. Stop plotting on how to get your way all the time. What is wrong with you people? Dismissed."

With that done I can move on to the next thing on my list. I feel a little better now that the meeting's over. Next is Mr. Sturmberger's photography class. I wait in the back until he nods to me. I slowly walk to the front and clear the burning phlegm from my throat. "This school is in dire financial straits. I want to keep this class. This class is well known at the state level. You will not find darkrooms in another school anywhere within a hundred mile radius. I also think it's healthy for your brains. And I like your pictures.

"But. But but but. I am seriously considering cutting this class because of the exorbitant cost of the chemicals needed to develop the film and photo paper. What I'm trying to say is: stop peeing the chemicals!" I pointedly stare at the back row of delinquent seniors. "Thank you for your time."

I am not five paces from the classroom door when I see Blake and Caitlin leashed together. I told them to stop doing that! It takes me just a moment to run back in the classroom and appropriate a pair of scissors from Sturmberger's desk and only half that time to run up behind the two and snip their leash. They spin around but when they see it's me they just glower and walk away. That will teach them. The leash doesn't look cheap.

At the northern border of the campus I double over and wait for my heart to return to it's regular beat. I get blurry vision. Sweat drips onto my shoes. I see that I'm standing on a water stained sheet of paper.

PRINCIPAL KENT SPOTTED AT RECOVERY ISLAND. That makes no sense. What is recovery island? Is it like rehab? There's no possible way the writer knows about my drug problem. No one knows. I hide it perfectly.

And now everyone knows regardless.

With no destination in mind I continue to run from the school until I black out.

When I come to it's 7:30. I have to come back to Bayview at 8:00 for a PTA meeting. Parents will be there, needing to be placated. Faculty will be there, exploiting any visible signs of weakness. I'm not worried or afraid, just tired. A quick line off my desk fixes that right quick.

I'm only ten minutes late. I try to make light of the situation but the meeting quickly goes south. A few parents complain about some other parents' children possibly exposing their own children to illegal drugs and becoming addicted. Some others take personal offense and start throwing accusations back.

"Don't talk to me about addictions!" I want to yell at the top of my lungs. "You are addicted to valium. I can tell by your posture and glassy eyes. And you are addicted to cigarettes. I can smell it from here. Couldn't make it five minutes, could you? Did you even enjoy it? Of course not! And *you* just can't wait until you're driving back home and

84

can crack open a beer on the way back. Who doesn't have an addiction?" But I just wait for them to tire themselves out as I would a group of crying toddlers. Where's Chris? I need desperately to do the phone call maneuver.

Some other idiot parent complains that her child told her that I went on an offensive anti-organized-religion tirade in her class that lasted many minutes. I don't remember this, but there have been more and more gaps in my memory as of late. "She may have found it offensive, but I assure you it was strictly educational and all sides of the issue were presented."

Later I hide in the bushes outside the front doors and watch the parents and teachers leave. Koont is the last to leave. I knew she would; she walks like a crippled mummy. I don't see Tyler's parents. I didn't expect them to attend the meeting but I was prepared for an altercation out here afterwards. I feel disappointment.

I walk to my house at a slower pace than usual. All I have to look forward to is a night of restless insomnia spent alone with my paranoia. Someone's waiting at my front door. I prepare for the fight I so desperately crave.

It's Sera. "My parents got in a fight. If I can't talk with you right now I'm running away. Tonight."

"Like, running away from home?"

"Running away from this whole *fucking city*." She swears like no one I've heard. I can see the expletive in glowing neon between us. Not really. It goes away after I rub my eyes.

"I'm very tired."

"Can we talk for just for a little while? Please?"

"... Alright."

We both sit where we ate the M&Ms. The wrapper's still on the carpet. She's got a paper bag in her hand I didn't see when I let her in. The water bottle she pulls out contains some sort of orange liquid. I see a small clown fish swimming inside but that turns out to be my imagination because it disappears after I blink. "What's that?"

"Orange juice. You look sick. You need some vitamin C."

"Okay," I say. That's very nice of her. I take a gulp. "Ugh. What kind of orange juice is this?"

"It's fortified. With vitamins."

"It stings a little bit. What kind of vitamins?"

"Just drink. You'll feel better."

Soon the bottle's mostly empty and the contents slosh around pleasantly in my guts. I feel woozy but warm. "There's definitely a stigma, or there was a stigma, I don't know if there is anymore... the tighty whities. The tight jockey underwear? All the cool kids wore boxers, I seem to recall, and they'd make fun of the other kids, like they were too embarrassed to ask their parents to buy them boxers, not like it was actually more comfortable. Which is debatable. So... I guess what I'm asking is, is there some sort of rift, like growing rift between groups of girls, y'know...."

"Yeah. In the locker room sometimes it's a big deal who's wearing 'slutty' underwear. Not all the time. It's stupid, anyway."

I forget how we got on this topic. "Hey Sera? What's recovery island?"

"It's some TV show. Everyone at school watches it. There's some island in the Mediterranean that's like one big rehab facility. It's in the middle of those crazy tiny party islands in the mediterranean. People who get fucked up everywhere close by stop there to sober up before going home. The show's just a bunch of reality TV bullshit. Bunch of messed up celebrities." No!

"Rehab! I don't need rehab! What are they saying about me?"

"Who's saying what about you?"

"I'm asking the questions! What are they saying? What do they know?" I shout everything. I can't help it. Someone else is moving my lips and saying these words.

"I don't know. Please stop yelling at me!"

"I can yell at you if I want!"

Sera moans like I just punched her. She covers her face and cries.

What am I doing? I'm a monster. "I'm so sorry."

"I came here to get away from the yelling," she sobs, her voice muffled by her perfect hands.

"I can't tell you how sorry I am. I... I have to confesh. I have a drug problem. I don't want the school to know. I have to look strong even though I'm weak. I'm so... weak."

She keeps gulping air. I rub her back gently until she stops. "It's okay. It's okay. I don't know what I was saying."

She hiccups. Her eyes look like lakes, deep green lakes. "You have a drug problem?"

I feel like telling her everything I can't tell anyone else. "Ahh, who doesn't? Anyway, I'm getting it under control. I shouldn't have raised my voice like that. I'll never do it again. Ever."

"I'm sorry I made you break your sobriety," she whispers. I can barely hear her.

"You don't even need to talk about it. Wait. What do you mean you made me break my sobriety?"

She points at the empty bottle. "That's basically straight vodka. I just put in enough juice to make it orange."

That explains why the room spins with increasing violence as I listen to her voice. "That's totally okay. Don't tell anyone, but I was hardly shober when I got here." I appear to be in a horizontal position now.

I feel her pushing me. "Lie on your side, you lightweight."

The carpet feels so soft. "Okay." I hear the door close. It sounds like it's many feet away.

When I wake it feels like God is driving an iron spike into my forehead.

15.

As much as it pains me I have to admit the county jail is almost as clean as my school. I stop scratching when Tyler sits down on the other side of the glass. I pick up the black phone receiver on my side and he picks up his.

"Are you okay, Tyler? Are you hurt?" He doesn't look any different, truth be told. Maybe thinner and unkempt, but other than that he's just as I remember him.

"Jesse said I shouldn't talk to you. He says you're the Devil."

"What do you think?"

"I don't think you're the Devil. Maybe just a satanist."

"Are you okay?"

"As okay as I can be after being framed for murder. You do remember doing that, right?"

I idly glance at the sign above us that reads *All Conversations Monitored and Recorded*. "I do not recall doing that."

He punches the glass so fast I only see it on the way back. The resulting sound is a dull thud. I flinch.

We sit in silence until I can't hold it in any longer. "Who's the third man?"

"The third man?"

"Who's writing the Gazette now? Who's your accomplice?"

Tyler smiles. "Wow. That's pretty fucking funny."

"You need my help. If you tell me, I'll help you. I can get you released. I'm testifying at your trial!"

"You mean you'll pin it on Jesse. You don't understand this, I'm sure, but for some reason I don't feel like betraying my best friend."

"Please. Who's writing the Gazette? It's driving me crazy. I don't know what I'll do if they write another issue. I don't know who I'll hurt."

"Are you saying you've hurt people before?"

I look up at the sign again. "Now that I know you've kicked your drug habit, I can honestly say I'm proud of you. You must stay clean. I know how easy it is to procure illicit substances in lockup. Focus on improving your business literacy and vocational skills. This doesn't need to be the end of your life."

"You know what Jesse says?" Tyler asks, examining his bruised knuckles. "He says the cops have no case. Once we're free, we're going to get you put in federal prison forever." If I was feeling even a little guilt before I came in here, it evaporates as soon as he stops speaking, along with any doubts that everything I do is just.

"I may be the Devil, but you're just a scared little kid." Somehow Tyler manages to hang up before I do. He spits at me. It hangs right in front of my nose. This place may look clean, but as long as Tyler and Jesse are in here it's filthier than the pipes under Bayview's bathrooms.

Involuntary thoughts of Bayview money troubles crackle in my brain once I'm back and I have a stark vision of rusty chains wrapped around my front doors. Chris reminded me today that we have very few options left. The time to decide which positions to cut is now. Now that I've accepted this brutal reality, the decisions become clear, if not necessarily easier to stomach.

First I visit the speech therapist. I watch Marinda Ulinski help Ivan Starks overcome his vocal impediment one excruciating word at a time and I can't bring myself to consider firing her. The same with the guidance counselors. Every student I see enter their offices leaves looking inarguably better no matter how problematic their previous behavior. Jeff Shasta the career counselor seems equally invaluable. He seems to produce scholarships out of thin air for my students. He helps them get to college with methods I can't even fathom.

School psychologist Robert Brown doesn't fit in with the rest of them, however. Why does Bayview need a psychologist if we already have such professional and devoted guidance counselors? If no good reason to keep him pops up this week, he's gone.

I find myself back in Chris's office. I wait until he can take a break from crunching numbers. "Chris, I don't know what to do. No matter what I come up with, it's not enough. What other options could we possibly have? Anything, no matter how improbable it seems."

Tapping his fingers on the desk, he quickly fires back, "We could have a silent art auction. We could maybe institute pension cuts. If we're feeling hopeful, we can start a campaign to repeal Proposition 8 and increase our cut of the state's property taxes."

"How quickly would we be able to do those last two things?"

"It would take years."

"But it will balance the budget?"

"Maybe," he states in a monotone. I don't know what's worse, my physical stress or his jadedness. "I've got to get back to this. Oh," he slaps his forehead, "Mrs. Relstab just sent a student to your office. Drugs, apparently."

I know how to handle this. I need this. I need to feel like I can succeed at something. I need to know I still have it. The touch. "Thanks Chris. Be strong."

He flexes his biceps. "Always."

Oddly, Mrs. Relstab and her student wait outside my office. This must be very serious. "Come in."

"I can't stay, Adam. I just wanted to let you know in person that when I was doing the random backpack searches you instituted, Cody here was found with an amount of... white powder in his backpack. It could be flour, or something else legal. But it's in this tiny plastic baggie." I stare at it after she places it on the desk. "Your problem now. I thought for sure he was a good kid." And she's gone.

This can't be happening. It isn't possible. I try to keep my thought in sequential order, but I'm torn between anger at Cody for violating the rules and anger at myself for feeling glee at receiving free drugs when I'm running low.

"I will not have drugs in this establishment, cookie stealer!" To show how serious I am I shout as loud as I can, knowing that nothing will escape the soundproofed walls.

"Uh... Mr. Kent. Your nose..."

I wipe away what feels like snot and my fingers come back stained with blood. That's unfortunate. Had to happen eventually though. Rusty pipes. Comes with the territory. I let my nose bleed. Cody is unnerved, to say the least.

"Don't say anything. Just listen to me. Can you do that?" Nod.

I say, "Brandon Nelson." No reaction.

I say, "Wes Peterson." His face tightens up as if he just got zapped with a hundred volts.

There's no question that the blame for Cody's situation lies with me just as much as it does with Wes. This all ends today. "You're expelled. Good luck getting into Central or Lincoln High. You disgust me." He knew he was expelled as soon as he was brought in here. He actually seems to relax. I guess the anticipation of punishment is sometimes worse than the punishment itself. I need to clean myself up.

After washing up in the restroom I take a moment to check my reflection. For a second my eyes look all inky black. Not just the iris and the pupil but the whole thing. I blink and it still looks like that. I know I'm just hallucinating from the drug abuse or maybe the lack of sleep, but it looks so real I feel a little off balance.

The hallucinations actually pay off in a way because I leave the bathroom at just the right moment to stop a group of five boys sprinting through the hall.

"What's going on guys?"

"Vince Maralia beat up his girlfriend. I guess that's a regular thing for him. We're going to beat him up so he knows what it feels like!" These are boys after my own heart.

"I don't disapprove, but please let the security guards handle this. I don't want to expel you fine gentlemen as well." They're crestfallen, and my heart goes out to them, but they do as they are told. Mike the security guard runs by, and the look he gives me translates to something like, "I got this". The system still works. Vincent is going *down*.

Chris approaches me from out of nowhere flanked by two gentlemen in tailored three piece suits. "Chris!" I say. "Did you hear about-"

"Yes, I did. The security guards have it under control. Adam, I'd like you to meet Mr. Morgenstein and Mr. White. They work for an independent agency that specializes in fixing financial situations like ours."

I don't have time for this. I need to hunt that abuser down. I feel the urge vibrating in my ribcage. "Hello... gentlemen...."

"We can privatize this school tomorrow, Principal Kent." At least they get right down to business. "Everyone is okay with it, all the way to the top. The Superintendent, the Board, the Trustees, everyone. Not only that, but we'll invest the proceeds for you. We guarantee returns."

Enough of this. It's time to hunt. "You know, I did some research on people like you. Did you know that in this year- in every year, actually- investment bankers lost some amount of the money they were given 50% of the time? I think I'll invest the money and take the 50/50 chance on myself. And that way if the money just disappears as money tends to do when it's around you people," I mouth the word "poof" and splay my hands, "I know what sort of magic trick is responsible."

The men nod. "Nice to meet you, Principal." When they shake my hand their gold watches catch the light just so.

"Sorry Chris. But I won't cross that line."

"Whatever. It was a long shot anyway. Those skuzzy guys would probably just take the money and run." He almost believes his own words. I see that his back is as straight as ever when he walks back to his paperwork. The true professionals remain unbroken even in the face of insurmountable odds. I'll have a better shot tracking down Vince in my monitor room instead of running around headless chicken style like my security guards tend to do.

Five screens show only static now. I try to look for Vince but I see that white face in the static no matter how I focus my vision. It's got black blood coming from its mouth. I do manage to catch the sight of Blake and Caitlin connected by a new leash hidden in the shade under the quad's oak trees. It's so obvious now that their relationship is healthy. Why is the good in people never visible until it's juxtaposed against the evil? The white face looks like a clown with its impossibly wide smile. Never seen a clown with black paint around empty black eyes, though. Maybe it's actually a skull.

In the middle of the bottom row of monitors I see two of my black-jacketed security guards dragging Vince through the quad. Nearby students throw food and trash. Disappointment is all I feel when I see this. Gripping his life in my hands was a boost I could have really used today.

I throw open the door to my office and close it behind me in one motion. Head cheerleader Erika Devine is inside twisting her chewing gum around a finger. She stands up and runs her hands along her jeans. "I don't feel very good about this, Mister Principal."

"What are you doing-" She interrupts me with a shriek and faints. I manage to catch her before she falls to the ground. "What's wrong?"

I immediately doubt the authenticity of the faint. She lifts her feet up onto her chair so I'm now supporting her entire weight with my arms. "No, Mr. Kent, no...." she groans. As she twists and struggles she grinds her lower back in a clockwise direction.

"Stop it Erika! Right now!" I can't drop her like luggage! I try to push her legs safely back onto the floor.

"Oh, Mr. Kent. Why are you doing this? Why?" Now she grinds in a counterclockwise direction. Her jeans begin to slip, but not enough. Not enough to see what I need to see, I mean, not "not enough" like I want her pants to slide down more, I mean... I do, but....

"STOP IT!" I shout. I only have one arm supporting her back because I'm trying to get her feet back on the ground so it's easy for her slide one hundred and eighty degrees and start rubbing her shirt in a side to side motion against mine. It feels like she put two ball bearings or something in there.

"Say *please*," she coos.

I drop her onto the carpet. The impact produces a muffled thump.

"Fine," she pouts from down there. After slowly standing up she pulls up her underwear unnecessarily to an unnecessary height for an unreasonable amount of time while she chews on her lower lip. Finally she snaps it back into place. "I feel so violated," she whispers, stretches, and then strides out the door.

And then I wake up. I'm still in the monitor room.

Did I just have a sexual dream about one of my students? Is it because the coke is eating holes in my brain? I don't want this. I'm better and stronger than this. I'm not a pedophile. I'm **not**. A sociopath, maybe, but there's a big difference.

I can't get a grip on my thoughts long enough to string two of them together. Fortunately the rest of the day is uneventful except for the final five minutes. Right before the end of the school day I hear a rumbling among the students that there's going to be a girl-on-girl altercation somewhere on campus very soon. We haven't had a catfight here in years! Violence I can deal with.

I get a gut feeling that it will happen on the basketball courts, and sure enough when I get there Amanda Christiansen and Eva Green are slapping at each other's faces and pulling at one another's hair. Everyone's doing the usual routine of standing in a circle and yelling for them to stop while making no actual move to stop it themselves. Of course I should stop it now, but often it's better for this kind of thing to play out for a while so all that pent up energy gets released.

They've taken to the ground now, as is common. Eva grabs Amanda's hair and bangs Amanda's head into the blacktop once and cocks back to do it again. I guess I've waited a little too long, we seem to have reached the endgame already.

"Okay, break it up, you two," I say in an authoritative tone as I restrain Eva from slamming Amanda's skull a second time. I can't imagine what it would be like to get in a fight with somebody while having long hair. Such a disadvantage! "What's this all about anyway?"

All Eva will say is, "She's a fucking bitch."

The bell rings and I have to leave it at that.

Hidden behind the bus stop I watch Wes talk and high five the students getting off the bus. Cody got off at this stop before I expelled him. Thinking that a drug dealer would follow any kind of agreement was a mistake. Trust no one who makes a living off of selling children addictive poisons.

I walk right up to him and push him in the chest, hard. Time so demonstrate who the boss is.

"You can't sell here anymore. Not at my school, not on this side of town. In fact, if I see you in the city limits again I will mess you up. Permanently." I push him again, daring him to make a move.

"Okay, okay! Don't trip! Let me call my boss. You guys can work this out, come to an arrangement and whatnot. Leave me out of this." Wes pulls out a cell phone and dials. He does continue to impress me with his business sense. *You don't want me. You want my boss.* And he's completely right. I want his boss right here, right now. After he makes the call we wait without discussing anything else. Especially not the school, or my job, or when exactly after he graduated that he went too far down the wrong path.

In no time at all the man I saw Wes do the handshake with drives up in a white Cadillac and leaves it idling as he walks toward me. His hands are deep in the pockets of that gray Harvard sweater so I don't know if he's armed.

"Hello, my name is Principal Kent. And you are?"

He shakes his head, hands still in his pockets. "I don't give a fuck what your name is! And as far as you're concerned my name is Jesus H. Christ. Wes, is this the guy who you've been slinging to?"

Wes nods. "Yeah, that's him."

"Where the fuck do you get off telling your *drug dealer* where he can and can't sell the shit you put up your nose on an apparently daily fucking basis?"

"When did you attend?" I ask, gesturing at his sweater.

He doesn't know what to make of that. "You better leave now, homie. You'll get your cut of the profit from Wes. Just go. Sit the fuck back and let him make you money." When I don't move a single muscle he rumbles, "You don't know who you're fucking with, Mister Principal."

"Why high school kids? I understand why people like you sell drugs to adults like me who should know better. But selling in a school zone? The criminal penalties are much worse. And my students are innocent- why are you trying to corrupt them?"

"Ha! Listen, dude, my deal is I sling to the upper-class white schools. This isn't the only city in my rotation, understand? I call it 'reverse neoliberalism'. If you all aren't aware of your invisible knapsack of white privilege and whatnot I'm going to jack it and take out all the cash you're not doing anything with. And there's nothing you can do about it. Accept it. This," he indicates the space all around us with both hands, which I now see are empty, "is not your school. Go back there. Go back in your hole."

"Or. What."

It's not a question, which finally makes him angry. "Or maybe later I will make you regret it." His empty hands, now fists, are still visible.

I try to appear confused. "Are you threatening me with violence now, or stating that you might threaten me with violence later?"

"I'm threatening you NOW you stupid motherfucker!"

I strike him in the face so hard when the back of his skull hits the ground his ankles shoot way up in the air. Violence I still know how to deal with.

"You don't-" I stomp on his testicles, "talk-" I kick him in the mouth and it makes a sound like a teacup breaking on cement, "to me-", a stomp to the testicles again, "like-" and finally a kick to the nose that pushes it way to one side, "that!"

He lies there like a corpse. I'm not even breathing hard. "You are mistaken. We are still in my school. And when you're in my school you treat the Principal with respect." I don't know if this nameless failure at life can even hear me right now.

Now I address Wes: "If I catch either of you in this city after today I will draw and quarter you. I'm not kidding. You can go drive your boss to the hospital now if you want, but I'd recommend that you catch the next bus out of here."

"Okay."

Wes drags the man's body into the backseat and peels away. Well, that's one problem solved. Is it starting to rain? I guess I need to change clothes. I'm chaperoning at Prom tonight.

I honestly don't even need to be here, which is oddly enough a very satisfying feeling. Everyone present is well behaved. The fast dances are frantic but relaxed. The slow dances are subdued and far too personal for me to have anything close to a full understanding of. It's very nice to just stand in the dark and listen to music while I watch young people quietly and respectfully make each other feel good. I want to be here forever.

Someone's inside my house. I can smell something unusual in the air as soon as I cross the foyer, like hibiscus. Sera! I feel like someone just granted me not only a stay of execution but my freedom.

She's in my bedroom. The bottom drawer of my dresser sits wide open and empty like the mouth of a cave and Ziploc bags lie in a pile at her knees.

"What have you done?" My voice is flint mixed with steel.

She almost screams. When she looks at me her large wet pupils remind me of a doe's. She looks more terrified than I've ever seen her. I've seen her sad, I've seen her scared, but I've never seen her vulnerable until now.

"What have you *done*?"

"It was raining! I, I was just looking for some dry clothes!"

"You can't do this. You can't just come into my house like this. You can't go looking around without me here. You messed up, Sera. Badly. Very badly."

Shamed, her gaze drops to the baggies from my dresser. "Are these all drugs, Mr. Kent?"

I respond with a defiant "Yes!" like I'm talking to some disapproving parent.

"Are you really trying to get better? Do you care about your sobriety at all?"

"Yes!"

"Do you even care about me?"

I can't bear to hear that question from her. "How can you ask that?"

No answer.

"Sera, what can I do to prove that I care about you?"

"Flush it all. Right now."

Oh dear. If I flush all the contents of the baggies arrayed in front of us I have no longer have a stash. And after the events of today I don't have a connection either. I'll be going cold turkey in a very brutal way. I didn't know my last hit would be my last hit! I would have made sure to enjoy it a lot more.

"Come with me," I mutter as I collect up the baggies. Sera may be scared and vulnerable right now but to her credit she doesn't hesitate before she follows me into the bathroom.

"This," I hold up a bag, "is crack. Believe me, fifteen second highs are not worth it." Pour. Flush. There's several hundred dollars gone.

Sera's irises have gone aquamarine.

"This is meth. Now meth, you can get high off meth for *days*. Especially if you don't sleep. You go a week without sleep you get way more high with the added hallucinations and euphoria. And psychosis. Meth psychosis is pretty sweet." Deep breath, pour, and flush.

Bye bye.

"This is DMT. Some people put it in an IV drip and do it that way." Flush. "This is heroin. Heroin is evil and more powerful than anything you can conceive of." Flush. "This is close to pure cocaine." Flush.

If Sera wasn't here right now looking at me without judgement I'd probably kill myself. Not commit suicide, but I'd probably get myself killed running through the city stealing from all the drug dealers I come across. "Lesson over."

"Do you want to listen to a song?" she takes out an electronic device and presses a button. Music bounces off the porcelain. Pretty good speakers for something so small.

"Who is this?"

"Spacemen 3. It's called 'Feel So Good'. Listening to it helps for coming down off stuff."

"How would you know?" I place my head on the toilet bowl. I want to vomit but my body won't let me. It's very frustrating.

"Just listen." After a while, it does make me feel, not good, but a tiny bit better. When was the last time I just sat and listened to music?

The song is over too soon. Sera's shoes tap on the tile. She's leaving.

"I'll be sober. For you. Only you. Okay?" My voice echoes in the toilet.

"Do it for yourself or it won't last very long. Please stop it. I don't want you to die, not from something you could have stopped."

It's nice to know that at least one person in this world doesn't want me to die. I'm not part of that category at the moment. I want to die instead of facing the cold morning alone.

16.

"A successful Principal must have a keen eye when fighting drug use at their school. Students can use rolled-up bills, hollowed-out pens and pencils, cut straws, long fingernails, Parliament cigarette butts, or even clean tampon applicators. Pay attention to the little clues. The are signs of larger problems."

I take a break from writing <u>The Principal's Guide to Success</u> to make another huge pile of chocolate-covered espresso beans on my desk. The trick to breaking the back of a stimulant addiction is to substitute a more socially acceptable and legal stimulant for the illegal and self-destructive kind you're currently addicted to. I crunch one between my teeth. It doesn't taste bad at all, and it might be my imagination but it actually seems to lessen the cravings somewhat. The problem with going cold turkey is that it often makes the side effects of chronic drug abuse worse. The beans help with my urge to get high, but it doesn't blunt the sharp headache, involuntary teeth grinding, or irregular heartbeat.

I can tell the knock at my door is Chris, but uncharacteristically he doesn't wait for my response before barging in. He looks at the mound of candy without comment.

"Do you care about Bayview, Adam?"

"...What?"

"By the way you ignore every piece of paper I give to you, it looks like you don't. It looks like you only care about yourself."

"How dare you!" I stuff a handful of beans in my mouth. "It's you who doesn't care! You're colluding with the enemy, aren't you? Chu, Koont, the Gazette, the school board? I know they're all linked, and now I see that you are too! Are you the mastermind behind all this, Chris? Are you trying take the throne? Hah! You wouldn't last a single day in my position!"

Chris suddenly looks broken. He leans back against my office door for support. "I don't want to be the Principal. I'm not like you. I'm not strong like you. Or maybe I just don't care about the students enough. I'm sorry I said what I did. I think you're the only truly moral person working at this school."

"That's not true. Any of it. You care about the student body as much as I do."

He still looks devastated. "Sometimes it's too much to fight against. The money, the rules, the teachers, the parents. Do you know what I mean? You and me, it's like we're trying to protect these kids from the whole world...."

"Chris, the only flaw you have is that you care too much about consequences." I stuff another mound of chocolate and caffeine into my mouth. Then I pat Chris comfortingly on the back and leave.

I've been looking forward to this since yesterday. I literally kick my way through Mrs. Koont's door and find her with only one other student. She's startled but recovers quickly. "My point being, Kelly, that if I see another OMG or LOL on one of your paper' again I will fail you without thinking twice. Understand?" I smile knowingly at Kelly as she rushes away.

"Mr. Kent! Ready to institute my undergarment policy changes?"

"Mrs. Koont?"

She smiles expectantly. "Yes?"

"Go have intercourse with yourself. Literally do that. I think your issue is that you don't do it enough. That's why you take it personally when boys don't want to look at you and have to get off on humiliating the people they're actually attracted to. You can't stop high schoolers from getting erections. Now please leave the school, walk into the nearest nursing home, and just go crazy."

One look at her face kills the cravings for a good thirty minutes. I wish I had it on tape.

I enjoy the temporary lack of pain and discomfort by going out into the quad and breathing in the fresh morning air. Minutes pass. I almost feel the peace I did at the big game against Lincoln High that happened an eternity ago.

The sound of paper blowing across the ground pulls me out of my reverie. There's at least twenty pages scattered along the ground. I pick one up and the itching comes back with a vengeance. PRINCIPAL KENT SEEN WITH FOUR NEW GIRLFRIENDS. The four pictures underneath the headline are the school photos of four female students I've never even touched once. Ever. I think back on Chris's words. Now I feel like the whole world is against me, too.

In my office I chew handful after handful espresso beans. The bitterness of the dark chocolate and coffee still calms me down a bit. It doesn't regulate my heart's rhythm unfortunately. Ginny the office lady buzzes me on the intercom: "Diana Kelly is asking to see you, Adam."

I try to find a place to hide the pile on my desk but quickly decide against it. "Send her in, please. Thank you Martine."

Diana's a petite sophomore with an excellent GPA and a bright future. I give her all the attention I have that isn't being spent on keeping my teeth from scraping against each other. "Diana! It's great to see you again! How can I help you?"

"I need to talk to you about my boyfriend. He's acting weird and I'm really worried."

"Who's your boyfriend?" I haven't added her to the string network.

"Tyrone Bailey." Ah, the student I affectionately refer to as the ticking time bomb.

"Diana, I don't think you need to worry about Tyrone acting 'weird'. He's got some issues regarding his parents and how he expresses his anger, but that's normal for a lot of people. He's seeing counselor Cindy and I have good, therapeutic talks with him whenever I can."

"You don't know him like I do. He's acting very weird. I'm scared."

"How is he acting?"

"Well," she takes a breath, "he's not talking to me. He's not saying a word to anyone. He's not even trying to fight anyone. He just keeps looking at his watch."

"There's nothing about what you said that should make you feel scared, Diana."

"Also, a couple weeks ago he said once that he was going to blow up the school."

My cravings stop. Time stops. Everything stops.

"I thought he was joking. And he probably was. Only... I've never seen him like this before!"

"Thank you for bringing this to my attention, Julia. Please remain calm and return to class. This will all be okay." I stop letting conscious thoughts dictate my actions. It's all instinct now.

I grab the first administrator I can find. "Evacuate the entire school immediately."

"But... but there's no fire drill planned. There's been no bomb threat!" Whoever he is, he's getting a pink slip tomorrow.

"We've had bomb threats written on the walls before and there's never a bomb. When it's the real deal they don't make threats. They just do it. So DO IT!" That gets him moving.

"And call the authorities!" I yell after him.

I go to the monitor room to make sure the children are streaming out of the building into the designated sections of the parking lots a safe distance away. My nose almost pressed to the screen, I continue to watch until I see Tyrone's familiar form. I hurdle down the hall through the river of students and find him.

"Can I talk to you for a minute, Tyrone? It won't take very long."

I lead him to the one room I know is being videotaped. Apparently I filled my pockets with chocolate before I left my office and I chew a fistful while he watches.

I swallow. "Hello Tyrone. Still seeing counselor Cindy on Tuesdays?"

His eyes are like opaque marbles. They don't seem to reflect the light. "Yeah. Why am I here?"

"Diana's concerned about you."

A genuine grimace. "What did she say?"

"I'm not going to tell you."

"What the fuck did she say?" he shouts.

"Are you going to hurt her? Are you like Vince Maralia?"

"No!" he tries to stand and I push him back down. He tries again and I push him down again. He's close to throwing a punch. "I would never hurt her. Never!"

"How do I know that? I want to believe you, but the evidence is against you. You think it's normal, right? Hitting the people you love. Your dad was abusive, right? Isn't that what you told your counselor?"

His eyes go wide. He's too shocked to take a swing at me now.

"That's why you're so angry all the time, right? That's why you beat up all those bullies, right? Do you still dream about it?"

94

He tries to stand again but I restrain him. "I see you think that violence solves everything. Did you learn that from your father?"

"No!" he roars.

"Did you even know your father?"

He goes rigid but I hold him down.

"No? So he left your mom when she had you, huh?"

"He died in the DESERT!" He's holding back tears. He's telling the truth.

"He died in the desert?"

He's making a sound that isn't quite sobbing. "He was going to come back in a week! He was almost out!"

Almost out? The desert?

"Tyrone, do you mean Iraq?" He can't hear me so he doesn't respond. He's talking only to himself now.

"And now that's all I see on the TV. That's all I hear the kids talk about. All I see is that motherfucking desert! Why did we go back? Why are our dads still going there to die?"

"I don't know. I'm sorry. What else do you see on TV?"

He's not looking or listening to me. I grab his chin and force him to make eye contact with me. "What else do you see?"

"IEDs. That's how everyone's getting killed. They're not getting shot, like my dad. They're getting blown up."

"You see car bombs? Do you see them when you're not watching TV?"

"Yeah. I dream about them. That why I had to...." He trails off, and he's not in the trance anymore.

"That's why you had to make one?" He shakes his head free from my grip.

Time for a little reality check. I whisper in his ear, "I'm a crazy man, Tyrone. You're not crazy; you're just damaged. *I'm* crazy. I'm a violent psycho."

He looks puzzled.

"Am I lying? Answer this one question and I'll let go: am I lying?"

"No. You're batshit insane."

I release him. He stays in his chair.

"I am. I'm not like you, or anyone else at this school for that matter. And I have no problem using violence to get what I want. I don't even think about it. I just do it. If you don't tell me which car it's in, I won't hurt you. I know threatening you with violence doesn't scare you.

"What I'll do is I'll hurt Diana. I'm not lying. I'll torture her. And I won't even feel bad. That's just who... I... am."

Pure terror replaces powerless anger on Tyrone's face. He's lost. I've won.

"It's the red Bug. The one in teacher parking."

Everyone's in the parking lot right now. They think they're safe. "When?"

"Pretty soon, Mr. Kent. You better go."

I'm already out the door.

Where's Chris? He knows how to contact all the teachers. They have emergency walkie talkies! Why don't I have one? What do I do?

"HELP!" The vacant halls echo my failure.

I get to the parking lot and there's no screaming. No explosion. "Get back inside!" I shout.

"But we just got here!" someone laughs. No one's paying attention. The teachers and students are talking as if this is some relaxing break from class. I've been here for eight years. When I want people to pay attention, they do.

"There is a bomb in the parking lot! If you don't get back inside you will all be BLOWN INTO LITTLE PIECES!"

At this, everyone starts running from the parking lot back into the building. I hope no one gets hurt or trampled. I creep forward until I see the car. I can't see what's inside.

Nothing happens.

It must all be one big hoax. One big senior prank. The real world hits my body all at once with the force of a sledgehammer. I fall to my knees, unable to breathe. Wetness runs down into my mouth and I taste blood. Cocaine nosebleed. Doubt grips my heart like a vice. I'm such an idiot!

When the car blows up it doesn't produce a big billowing pillar of fire and a long-lasting rumble like in the movies; that's what a gasoline explosion looks like. The vehicle just vaporizes into a gray cloud with a sharp *bang*. Metal and glass shrapnel shred the parked vehicles around me. I don't even see any fire.

The ensuing quiet is nice. A fire truck breaks it when it bursts into the parking lot, sirens blaring.

"The authorities are here. I'm so glad."

"Adam! Oh my God, are you okay? You're bleeding." It's Chris.

Am I? Nothing hurts... oh, right. "I'm fine, Chris. I just got a bloody nose when I fell down. Is anyone injured?"

"I don't think so. It's going to take a while before we know what's going on. Everyone's scattered all over the place. Can you come help me get make sure no one's missing?"

"I need a minute, Chris."

"I understand. Do you want me to go?"

"No." We watch the oily black smoke tower over Bayview. "One day I won't be fast enough."

"What?"

"One day I won't be fast enough. Or smart enough. One day I won't be willing to cross a line and everyone else will pay the price. These kids get smarter every day, and they are their own worst enemy."

Chris wordlessly hands me a tissue and I try and get all the blood and dirt off my face.

Eventually we get all the students safe and calmed down. For once, my employees do their job without explicit direction. Chris and I step back outside to survey the damage.

I smell smoke. Not the acrid smell of burning rubber. Cigarette smoke.

"Adam! What the fuck happened here? I'd think I was in the Goddamn middle east but I don't see anyone fucking a goat." He shakes Chris' hand. "Detective Cooper. Pleasure."

"What are you doing here, Detective?"

"Well, I felt like taking some time out of my busy schedule to come down here and give you some moral support, ha."

"Do you know who did this?" Superintendent Burnside wobbles up to me, somewhat plastered.

"Yeah, do we know who did this?" Cooper chimes in.

"Uh..." Chris glances at me. "Do we?"

I don't like having these three looking at me like this. "Yes. It was a student named Tyrone. He confessed."

"On tape?" asks Burnside.

"Yes, on tape."

"Wow! I'm fuckin' impressed, Adam. What, did you make him an offer he couldn't refuse?" Chris, Cooper and Burns laugh in unison and then stare at me when they realize I didn't laugh with them.

"What? C'mon man, it's the Godfather! Give me some credit!"

"Sorry, I don't watch the new TV shows."

Their jaws drop. "It's a *movie*."

"What will you charge him with, Cooper?" I ask.

"Oh, this isn't my case, I'm homicide. It's too bad nobody died." He waits for me to laugh. "Anyway, the regular cops are gonna be here soon. I'm just here to say... hi." He nods to the other two. "Bye now."

"Adam, is there anything you'd like to tell me about this? Can you enlighten me on what's going on?" Burnside is almost pleading.

"You heard what I told Cooper. That's all I know."

Burnside rubs his flushed face. "I feel like you're keeping me in the dark, Adam. Nothing I can do, though. Meet me in my office in ten. My superiors are here. They want to talk to you."

"I'll be glad to finally meet them," I say. I think it's the truth. "Can you handle this by yourself for a while, Chris?"

"Of course I can. Go do your thing." He reaches out a hand. "This wasn't a good day. But it could have been so much worse."

We shake. "Can I still have dinner with you? At your house?"

My VP smiles. "Next week. You need to give my wife and I some time to prepare." I feel embarrassed, but in a pleasant way. "Get some sleep. You've got raccoon eyes."

"So do you."

When I get to Burnside's office he introduces me to an immaculately dressed man and woman: Jackson and Burke. Their administrative positions are words I've never heard before, executive this and vice executive that. *I wish I could cut your salaries*, I think. I tell them what I know about the bomb and Tyrone. It takes less than five minutes. Afterward, they shake my hand.

"I can see you have this entirely under control. I wish all our Principals could be like you. Keep on producing those amazing numbers!"

That was easy.

I wait until the others are gone before I ask Burnside, "Have you been lying to your superiors about the budget, George?"

Burnside just shrugs, not even trying to defend himself. He pulls out a green glass bottle. "Want some scotch? You look like you could use some."

"No thanks. Trying to stay sober. You know, those two outrank you, but they actually look like they enjoy their job."

Burnside shrugs again and takes a long swig. "So do you. I don't understand any of you people."

17.

"A successful Principal follows all safety procedures and ensures that all others do the same. Every student is a tiny potential Chernobyl."

Caffeine isn't doing it for me anymore. I've already licked the entire surface of my desk, the monitor room, and that one handicapped stall. I can't focus. I'm in a state of constant pain.

But I'm still clean.

The students are shaken over last week's events but seem to feel safe again. To make sure of that I'm spending the day visiting classes and examining the students. The Physics classes are building catapults. The Chemistry classes are sublimating solids into gases. When I enter Bernard Maxwell's history class, they're talking about war.

"Why did we go to war in Iraq?" someone asks.

Bernard Maxwell looks bored. "Mr. Kent? Would you like to try and answer that?"

I find myself facing a class with absolutely no idea of what to say. Struggling for the right words pleasantly distracts me from the physical withdrawal symptoms.

"War is messed up, we can all agree on that. But what constitutes war? What constitutes an invasion? The Iraq war was technically an invasion since this country never officially declared war on Iraq. How many of you think it was right for this country to invade Iraq?" Three students raise their hands.

"Okay." Nothing else to say comes to mind until I remember a conversation I overheard between two of my teachers. "Who here knows about what happened recently in Libya?"

Jordan Hunt raises his hand. "Their president was killing his own people, so Europe and the US made a no fly zone so the people had a chance to fight back."

"Right. Good answer, Jordan."

"Ghaddafi got knife fucked," says Madeline Washburn. The class gasps.

"That's inappropriate language, Madeline. But please clarify what you mean, if you would."

"When the rebels caught Ghaddafi they shoved a knife up his rectum. I saw the video. They tortured him before they killed him."

"Correct," I say. "They did indeed. How many of you think that it was wrong for them to torture Ghaddafi?" Two students raise their hands. "How many of you think that this is proof that America brought democracy to the Middle East?"

No one raises their hands.

"I guess I don't know how to answer the question of why we went to war. Even if one day I understand why Saddam's hanging feels not quite right and Ghaddafi's torture feels so just, I don't think I'll be able to answer your question. I'm sorry I couldn't be any help." The itching is so bad I can't even wait until I leave the class before I start the vigorous scratching.

I sense a commotion in A-wing even though it's far away on the other side of the school. The first thing I notice when I get there is the crowd of students laughing and giggling outside Mr. Davidson's room.

"Everyone! Why aren't you in class, learning?" They just laugh. I walk inside. Mr. Davidson sits at his desk, his expression haunted. The floor is covered by a writhing mass of ladybugs. Hundreds are crawling up his desk, but he does not budge.

"Am I dreaming right now, Principal Kent?"

"No, Mr. Davidson. Why don't you go to the nurse's office right now? Also, you might want to pay more attention to your students. And stop telling them about your dreams."

The students quiet down when they see me lead Mr. Davidson away. "No one is in trouble," I say. "I'd just like to know how this was done."

"Maybe someone bought a bunch of frozen ladybugs from the pet store and left them in Mr. Davidson's desk overnight to thaw," squeaks Amy Hood. Wow, she's good.

"Thank you for the hypothesis. Please, no more pranks on Mr. Davidson this year. His psyche is extremely fragile right now. Okay?"

"Okay Mr. Kent!" they chorus.

The final bell rings. Is the day already over? That didn't seem excruciatingly long. Maybe the worst of the cold turkey symptoms are over. I walk back to the quad to make sure there aren't any new copies of the Gazette lying around and when I get there I find a group of drug dealers.

Harvard stands in front, satisfyingly bruised and bandaged. Wes hides behind him. Three other men stand to the side.

Harvard speaks first. "I've been watching you for a while, you fucking creep. What kind of sick fuck are you? You basically live here, you spend all your money on drugs, you bring little girls back to your house... I mean, I though I was a bad guy, but damn!" His henchmen giggle like little girls themselves.

"Wesley? What do you think you're doing?" I ask.

"I'm not a fucking kid, you prick! I'm not one of your students anymore! I'm gonna love watchin' what happens next!"

Harvard holds up a hand and Wes shuts up. "I waited until all the kiddies left because I'm a nice guy, believe it or not. I'm so nice I'm not even going to kill you. I'm just going to hurt you. A lot. All day and all night. And you won't do anything about it when I'm done!"

He sneers and I can see he already got his teeth fixed. "You know why? Because I can just as easily come back here when this place is brimming with innocent children and execute them all one by one." The man to Harvard's left pulls out a black Colt .45.

Eight shots, large caliber. Even if the first one doesn't kill me, it'll put me down for good.

"You can execute *that* student if you want," I say, pointing. All of them look, and the man with the gun absently points it at the ground.

I've closed the distance before they can turn back around. I grab the gunman's wrist with both hands, break it easily, and kick the falling gun away. Then I break his jaw with my elbow and throw him to the pavement. He's down for good.

"Get that motherfucker!" yells Harvard. The other two nameless goons run at me when they should have walked. The first one I trip and he falls hard, and when the other reaches me I just flip him over my back. The man who I tripped tries to get up and I step hard on his neck. The second man gets up faster than I expect and his fingers suddenly close around my face from behind so I snap my head back. I feel and hear his nose snap against my skull and when he lets go of me I spin and kick him in the genitals. When he sinks to his knees I kick him in the side of the head.

Harvard sprints towards the gun and I do too. He gets to it before me but he fumbles at it too long and can't seem to pick it up.

Nerves.

I tackle him, get on top, and force back his arms with my knees. Then I pound him in the face over and over and over again until it doesn't look like a face at all.

I pick up the gun. It's heavy. Wes should be trying to run right now but he's just standing there, petrified.

"On your knees."

He drops to prayer position. I put the gun against his head.

"You want to be treated like an adult, do you Wes? Do you want to see how I treat adults? DO YOU?"

He screams in terror, "No! I'm sorry Principal Kent! I'm sorry!"

It was smart of him to call me Principal. "Give me your phone."

I use it to call the police. The gun stays at Wes's temple. "Keep in mind that you are an ounce of finger pressure away from death."

I really should have expected Cooper to show up first. He didn't even have time to light one up before got here, apparently. "What the fuck is all this? Are you seriously getting in a brawl now, at the school, with the trial so Goddamn close? You're supposed to be my immaculate witness!"

He sees the gun in my hand. "Woah! Where'd you get that big bastard? Did you get it from these guys?"

I extend it out for him to take, grip forward. He takes a step back.

"This right here?" I continue holding it out for Cooper to take. "This doesn't make me look bad. It makes me look like a superhero. I'm saving this school from demons every day. What do you save anyone from?"

"Don't come back here. I don't want to see your greasy face until the day of the trial. Call my office when you actually know the date."

Cooper is taken aback at first. Once he recovers he quickly lights one up and blows the smoke in my face. "Well fuck you then, cunt. Just trying to be friendly."

"And you can afford more than one suit!" I yell at his retreating form. I think he would have flipped me the bird if the real cops didn't decide to drive right past him at that moment on their way to clean up my mess.

Chris has a very nice house. The interior is clean and spacious, there are bookcases and vases and potted plants in just the right places, and there are pictures of his kids everywhere. And his wife is very attractive, which always adds to the ambiance.

"Thank you for dinner, it was delicious!"

"I'm so glad you came, Adam. Chris talks about you all the time." Vanessa sweeps back her hair and winks at her husband.

"Good things?"

"Sometimes." We all laugh at that, except the one child present who isn't old enough to say words yet. "My it's late. Time for bed, guys!"

The children complain and protest that they want to stay up and play with Mister Principal but she manages to herd them up the stairs pretty quickly.

"Let's go in the living room," suggests Chris.

"If I can move," I half joke. I'm so full it feels like I've doubled my body weight.

We both sink into a plush couch and gaze at the flickering fireplace. "So what happened at the school today?" Chris inquires.

I rest my head on the tall back of the couch. "Nothing you need to worry about. A few drug dealing gang bangers intruded on school grounds looking for some student to sell narcotics to."

"Were they stupid enough to have the drugs on them?"

"A couple were. I think that's how the boss paid them. He should've hired some professional muscle and not a couple of his junkie customers. It's fine. I took care of them."

"Are they still alive?"

"Yeah."

A minute passes and Chris says, "We did it."

"Did what now?" The flames are mesmerizing.

"We bought the school another fiscal year. With three weeks to spare!" He raises his arms in victory, then winces and holds his stomach.

I can't believe it! "How did you do that? There's no way the changes I made were enough! All I ever saw you do in your office was write down numbers. You never even used a calculator!"

Chris just smiles.

After watching the fire for a little while longer, Chris says, "Can I be upfront with you?"

"Always."

"Never have kids."

I wasn't expecting those words to come out of his mouth. I'd believe he said he moonlighted as a transgender prostitute before he said something like that. "You look so happy! I wish I-"

"Don't." I shut up. "I bet you came in here and all of a sudden you wished you had kids, right?"

"How'd you know?"

"When I say don't have kids, I don't mean you personally. Just some general advice. You may think your life suddenly gains meaning when you have a baby, but that doesn't happen. You need to make your own meaning out of life or else you'll never find it."

I want to ask more questions but Chris shushes me. Venessa's coming down the stairs.

I don't make it to my house until about midnight but when I get there the lights are on. "I told you that you can't just walk into my house like this," I mutter. "But I guess

I don't lock the door either."

I walk inside and Sera's smile makes me feel so good I break down crying.

"Adam! Why are you crying?" I'm on my hands and knees and can't even look at her. I just let the tears come. She doesn't ask again; she just cradles my head in her hands.

When I can talk again I gulp, "I almost killed a student today. One of my kids. I almost killed them. I was so close to doing it."

"But you didn't."

"No," I gasp. "I've never killed a student. I've killed people, though. More than one."

"They deserved it."

"You don't know that!"

"No, but I know *you*."

"I just want everything to go back to the way it was when everything made sense."

"You can't make things go back to the way they were until you go back to the way you were."

"You're the only good thing in my life anymore. Is there still hope for me to be a good person? Can I change?"

"I think you already have and you just don't know it yet."

I wish she could hold me in her arms until I died. "I have really bad insomnia. I can only sleep when I'm around you. Did you know that?"

She takes her hands away. "Don't make me your validation. I'm not going to be your only reason for being sober. I'm not going to be your only reason to live. That's your job, you fucking asshole."

"You're right." She puts her hands back. "When I'm with you, I don't feel like the Principal. I feel... safe."

"Do you like this? Where we are right now?"

"Yes. Of course I do."

"Is this okay, me being here?"

"Yes."

"... is this okay?"

"Is what okay?"

"..."

"Oh. Oh yes."

18.

"A successful Principal does not fear jail. A successful Principal does not fear death. Do not let the threat of jail or death sway you. Let nothing sway you but your students."

I wrote a whole chapter of the <u>Guide</u> today. The words come slowly but they come strong. It feels good to write again.

I will end the Gazette today. I can feel the truth of this in my bones. It will all end today. I just need to get "old school". Things can't go back to the way they were until *I* go back to the way *I* was. I just needed clean myself up and for someone to show me the way out. I will end the Gazette today.

The question now becomes: what did I used to do when I needed to fix a problem like this? I can't remember. I can't remember.

Maybe I should check the security cameras. There's hours upon days upon weeks of footage archived in there. The Gazette writer must be in there somewhere.

However, after gazing at the screens in the monitor room for a minute it becomes clear that only one camera still works. Every monitor except the one at the top is static. That one still films the front entrance from above the double doors. Huh. Someone's replaced the mascot! I stare at the other screens' static trying to catch a glimpse of the white-faced demon that used to lurk there, but all I see is snow. Wow, it's nice to be clean.

I could still watch the archived footage if I want, but now that I'm here I no longer have the desire to. I didn't have cameras at Bayview for seven years, and then as soon as I buy them everything goes down the toilet. Coincidence? Maybe. But the answer won't be found in here. Anyway, it's enough that the students think the cameras still work.

I know: the evidence room! That's a blast from the past. I haven't been inside in a long time.

The air inside the room smells sweet and familiar. Running my hands along the shelves, they come back caked with dust. I guess it's time for me to start confiscating things again. In a dark corner I find a cardboard box overflowing with handwritten notes I've collected off the ground or from the students themselves. I need to immerse myself in the candid lives of my students. Even if I don't find the answers I want, it will make me feel good. It might remind me of my purpose.

Somewhere in the middle of the box, a note catches my eye. One person wrote a question on it, and someone else wrote a one word answer. That's all. It's small and easy to miss. I want to put it aside but something in my gut won't let it go. I compare it to the handwriting on another note.

Then I'm in front of the network of pink and blue string that represents every romantic connection at Bayview. It's both beautiful art and hard science at the same time. And it's love, too. I trace a path from one pin to another. Eventually I reach a gap that shouldn't be there. It doesn't fit with the pattern. I examine the note again. I recall a fight between girls, not the last one, but the one before that....

And then a synaptic lightning bolt a million miles long hits me and my heart breaks for real.

The note in my hands reads "Do you want to go out with me?" and "YES".

It's 7:00 PM and I'm watching the last football game of the season. I can't see the score because the scoreboard is covered with so many ads the numbers aren't visible. Let them complain.

I have to leave at 8:00 PM because there's a five year reunion tonight I must attend. One of my first crops from my time as Principal. Everyone's dressed nicely. I can tell than some are bitter about their four years here. Some are just hollow husks already, brought low when the world presented its brutal truth to them. Some are successful in one way or another and are here to relive their time here or visit old friends or laugh at those who aren't so successful. Some came here to remember and now they have to drink liquor very fast when they figure out that remembering this school is the last thing they ever wanted. The drink ticket system is an obvious farce. Everyone's helping themselves to the bar and getting far too inebriated. Also, someone partially hollowed out a melon and poured alcohol in so when it finally ended up here it looks like just a melon but it's actually saturated with vodka. Thus, many of my students are now dancing with each other in an inappropriate fashion. And I let them.

Why wouldn't I? For one night they're only my students partying against the darkness that lies just outside my walls.

The lights are on when I finally get to my house. Someone's home.

I make sure to enter the house silently. I watch Sera in the kitchen. She's brought a hot plate and she's cooking something. It smells like heaven.

"Hi Mr. Kent!" She doesn't turn around. "I'm making you some food! I hope that's okay. You're too skinny!"

"Sera, I'd like to do something with you right now."

She takes the pot off the heat and places it carefully on the counter. Then she finally meets my eyes with those emerald reflecting pools. "Anything."

"I want us to write down our reasons for living. I've already written one of mine down." I show her the paper in my hand. It says "Sera".

Her eyes glitter. "I'll tell you mine. Why don't *you* write it down, though?"

"Because I want to see your handwriting."

Suddenly she has a small black canister out in one hand and she's backing away from me. "Don't come any closer."

I raise my hands up and show them to her. "I'm just going to stand here. I swear. Let's just talk. Okay. I'll stay right here."

She takes another step towards the back door. "You know why I cried that night? My parents weren't fighting! I was scared of YOU!"

"I would never hurt you. Never. Let's just talk. Please. Why did you make me flush the drugs, Sera? That could have been evidence against me. Why did you get me sober?"

"I know everything you did! I can prove it! I'm going to the police right now!"

"I don't care. Please. Let's just talk. You can do whatever you want after this. I just want to know how many dates you and Tyler went on before you FUCKED HIM!"

"I hate you!" She's crying now.

I take one step towards her. "Yeah? Why did you save my life, then? Why did you save my life if you hate me so much?"

"If you take one more step I swear to God I will pepper spray you."

I take another step. "Sera, I love-"

Suddenly I can't breathe or see. I lunge forward and soft hair bushes against my fingers. I try to wipe out my eyes and run after her at the same time. I hit the door and break through it into my front yard. The night air burns my lungs. I smell hibiscus, maybe, just for an instant.

A car starts right next to me. I slam my fist into what feels like the window but the glass doesn't break. I hear her scream inside. I try to find the door handle but the car accelerates too fast.

The car's gone. Now all I smell is burning rubber.

"SERA!" I scream. "SERA!" Can she hear me?

When I can see and breathe again I make a plan of attack. She's going to the police station, that's what she said. There's more than one in this city, but she's going to drive to the closest one. If I can get there before she does, somehow, I can see her again. And do what?

It's hopeless. I start running anyway.

Her car isn't in the nearest police station's parking lot. She wouldn't have gone to the police somewhere else. Where is she? Did she decide not to turn me in? I don't dare to hope. She could have gotten here in ten minutes flat if she was driving fast enough. If she was....

Not that. Anything but that.

I run to the Ash Street intersection faster than I've ever run before. The paramedics are there, gathered loosely around a twisted burning hunk that used to be a car. Why didn't she slow down at the turn? Why didn't every single person who died in this exact spot slow down just a little bit?

"Please!" I scream at the closest person dressed in white. "I'm her family! Is she alive? Is she breathing?"

"They just took her to St. Jacob's. She was breathing when they pulled her out of there, that's all I can tell you."

I should be strong and go to the hospital right now. Better yet, I should go to the police and turn myself in. But I'm not strong. I'm just tired.

Well, no use dwelling on the past. I'll deal with all this in the morning.

19.

"Every career must end. The hardest part of your career will be deciding when to end it. The easiest way for you to make this decision: work until you die."

It's not the last day of school for my students but their last day with me as their Principal. I wish I could come back. I'm wearing a jacket I forgot I stashed in my office years ago. It's long and black with lots of pockets and it keeps me warm as I walk around.

Nothing I see makes me sad. There's a girl teaching her friend dance steps. I see my Golden Couple holding hands. Everyone smiles at me. And there's no litter. Am I dreaming? No litter at all?

Chris runs up to me, out of breath. "Sera Roth is in the hospital. She was in an accident last night."

"Who?"

"Don't you know everyone here?"

"Not everyone."

"I can go down there if you don't want to."

"I'll go. Thanks for everything you've done for me, Chris. You're the best friend I ever had."

"What? I didn't hear the last thing you said."

"I said you'll be a fine Principal one day." He glows with pride.

I can't count all the tubes and wires hooked up to Sera's body. Her chest rises up and down. She looks at peace. Her parents are right next to her, looking at me with eyes that have no tears left.

"Adam!" Detective Cooper walks in. He's wearing an olive turtleneck and clean slacks. He looks like a different person.

"Why are you here?"

"I'm a friend of the family."

I know this will be the last time I see Sera. I want to feel her pulse and smell her skin. I can't touch her ever again and it kills me.

"Why aren't you getting any closer?" Cooper asks. "It's okay. It looks like she meant a lot to you."

"That would be inappropriate. All my students mean a lot to me. I'm sorry for your loss, Mr. and Mrs. Roth."

"She's going to wake up," her mother croaks.

"I know. It's a temporary loss." I just want to see Sera's eyes. That's all. But I have to leave.

"Goodbye." I look at her parents when I say this but it's only for her.

It's seventh period. I'm the Principal for another twenty minutes. There's one monitor left and I watch it without blinking. Four minutes left and I see Detective Cooper walk through the double glass doors with a uniformed officer in tow. He's wearing that nasty trench coat again. He walks straight to my office. I wait until they're both inside and then walk into the bathroom across the hall, adjacent to the room Cooper's in.

I enter the last stall and stand on the toilet. There's a grate next to me covering a ventilation duct and I press my ear to it.

"I know he's not in his fucking office! Tell me where he is! I know you know where he is!" Good thing he's shouting, it makes him much easier to hear.

"I can't do that because no one knows where he is!"

"See this photo? Do you know who this is?"

A pause. "Oh my God! That's a skull!" I hear retching.

"We found it buried in your boss's backyard. You don't know who this is? This is Principal Adam Kent. Don't you recognize him?"

Time to go.

I walk to the door but I stop when I smell cigarette smoke. Someone smoking in *my* restroom? I kick open the nearest stall and Brandon Nelson gawks at me. If I had time I would see justice done. Instead I just draw a finger across my throat and run out the door.

Cooper must have seen me run past because I hear him say "Heeeeeeeey Adam! Just the man I was looking for! Going somewhere?"

I look at him and flash a smile. "Detective Cooper. How's Sera?"

"Oh, she's fine. In fact, she was never even in a coma! I just needed you to come back to the hospital and see how you reacted. You're one cold son of a bitch, Adam. Or whatever the fuck your name is."

"You boss should have hired her to do your job. After all, she's the one who caught me."

The lady cop behind Cooper snickers.

I continue, "I was under your nose the entire time you were on this case, you failure! And I held your hand the entire way! I got you the coke dealer. I got you the car bomber. I even got you the person who killed the Ray Paba."

"YOU killed Ray Paba!"

I shrug. "Eh."

"Do you have any regrets?" the lady cop asks. I think about this for a moment. Good question!

I catch Brandon out of the corner of my eye. He's laughing and pointing.

"My only regret is not putting out that boy's cigarette on his tongue."

"Okay. That's it, motherfucker," Cooper snarls. The officer reaches for her cuffs. "You have the right to remain silent."

I reach into my pocket and throw the shuriken at Cooper's face. It sinks deeply into his left eye. Well made, Daniel.

The officer makes a move and I throw powdered glass into her face and punch her in the chin. Then I run for the exit. They're both screaming. Four more officers run in through the front doors towards me. They swarm me and I'm crushed under their weight. I almost can't move, but I find the strength to throw three of them off. The fourth cop I shove hard into the doors and they break into jagged pieces. Fragile things.

"Don't shoot! I want that cocksucker alive!" Cooper sounds more angry than hurt. I pass through the opening in the glass and taser wires pass over my right shoulder.

Out in the sun I jump and clear every single stair. Two cop cars sit empty in front of me and two more come screaming into the parking lot. I leap onto the roof of one of the empty cars.

This is nothing I haven't seen before. I have my escape route all planned out. The reinforcements will pop their tires on the nails I laid out after I got back from the hospital. In the meantime I cut to the right and disappear into the grove of oak trees nearby. That gives me time to switch directions and run along the perimeter of my school until I get to the sewer I removed the manhole cover from. Then I just emerge somewhere else in the city, steal a car, and I'm gone.

But that's only a fantasy. I'm still on the car when I feel three bullets hit home before I even hear the reports.

20.

"I did not write this guide for you. I wrote this guide for your students. Thank you for reading."

I guess I'm still alive. I wake up in prison. How long was I in the hospital? I don't ask anyone any questions. When I hear my charges read, I plead not guilty.

The trial takes at least a year. Maybe more. During the trial I find out that for years Superintendent Burnside took a portion of the assets side of the school's books and somehow converted it into cash which he then stored in his desk drawer next to his liquor. He took the money and ran, I suppose. He's gone. No one knows where he fled to. Wherever he is, I'm sure there's an open bar.

In the beginning I could look behind me and see people in the crowd I recognized. Chu. Cooper in his normal crusty clothes and stylish new eye patch. I hear he's writing a book about the "Bayview Psycho Principal". I see the trinity that formed my downfall: Jesse, Tyler and Sera. I see Chris, graying now at the temples, and his wife. Other students and faculty. Parents. My superiors.

After a while everyone I know stops coming. Now the room is entirely filled with well dressed strangers. Some take notes. I wonder what my friends are doing now. Getting on with their lives? Still talking about me? I wonder if, for them, did I even exist at all?

I disagree with certain charges. One in particular, of a sexual nature. I would make lengthy points regarding the age of consent in Italy and Nigeria and the rapid sexualization of the newer generations of humans, but those aren't relevant to my case.

I only ask, "Did she say we had sex? Did she?" and they won't answer. "Well, I'm saying we didn't, so I guess that's that!"

At the end of the trial I take the stand. Some professional people from some agency or another suggested that it would benefit me in the long run if I took the stand, drew the trial out and all that. Something about ratings and product placement and keeping people's minds off more pressing matters. I agree with their suggestion.

The prosecution asks the usual questions and then when I'm completely relaxed they throw a curveball.

"Is your real name Lloyd Dimon?"

"That's one of the names I have gone by, yes."

"Is that your real name?" I argue the definition of "real" and "name" until they give up. "When you lived in Colorado you went by the name Lloyd Dimon, correct?"

"Yes."

"Is it true that while you lived there you worked as a police officer and had a wife and two children?" I don't like how he groups all three questions into one.

"Yes."

"And is it true you ran for political office, mayor specifically, four times?"

"Yes, that is true."

"And is it true that the fourth time you ran for office your competitor, a Mr. Blankfein, won and was subsequently found dismembered along with several of his constituents?"

"No."

"The facts show-"

"It's true that Hank got chopped up. I'm not arguing with that. But Hank did not win. You don't win if you *cheat*. He stuffed ballots, he paid off the chamber of commerce, he defamed me and my family! Those who died were bought and paid for. No big loss."

"Did you kill them with an axe?"

"I won. Of course I didn't kill them. But I won."

"Did you murder Adam Kent?"

"Let's just say his death was better for everyone involved."

"Even for Adam Kent?"

"The things I saw him doing... I wouldn't call that a life."

My last remarks are directed towards my students, all of whom I can't see, "There's no such thing as the daily grind. Not if you love what you do."

Before I know it, the jury has reached a verdict: guilty on all counts. The sentence is life several times over. The gavel goes bang!

And now I'm here in my cell. In exchange for pleading not guilty and taking the stand, my only request was for a black silk tie. I carefully knot it at my throat and pull it tight.

I can see the bars of my cage and that is what makes me truly free. For people like me prison isn't a punishment, it's a dream come true. There are thousands of adult delinquents all around me who never got what they deserved from their public education. It's time for me to finally show them the difference between right and wrong. They will learn. My name is Prisoner #54471072. I am the Prisoner.

The bell rings. My door slides open. It's time for class to begin.

The End

Joseph Schumacher is a UC Santa Cruz graduate and currently resides in Orange County, California. He has worked as a writing tutor, parking attendant, paperboy, DJ, landscaper and pizza artisan. The Principal is his first novel.